In Hot Water . . .

Emily pulled off her sneakers and headed upstairs to take her shower. That was really nice of Jessie, she thought. She really is making an effort to make up for last week. It's like she's a changed person. I like this Jessie much better.

The hot water felt so good. Emily let it run through her hair for a long time. I could stay in here forever, she thought. It's so warm and steamy.

But she remembered that Jessie was waiting for her to come downstairs and help, so she finished shampooing her hair, washed quickly, and stepped out of the shower. Humming to herself, feeling very refreshed, she walked over to the mirror. It was steamed up, rivulets of water trickling down.

Emily picked up a towel and rubbed it across the mirror to wipe away the steam. She peered into the mirror.

Then she screamed.

And screamed again.

She had the feeling she might never stop screaming.

Books by R. L. Stine

Available from ARCHWAY Paperbacks

FEAR STREET
R·L·STINE

The Stepsister

AN ARCHWAY PAPERBACK
Published by POCKET BOOKS
New York   London   Toronto   Sydney   Tokyo   Singapore

AN ARCHWAY PAPERBACK *Original*

An Archway Paperback published by
POCKET BOOKS, a division of Simon & Schuster Inc.
1230 Avenue of the Americas, New York, NY 10020

Copyright © 1990 by Parachute Press, Inc.

ISBN: 0-671-70244-0

First Archway Paperback printing November 1990

20   19   18   17   16   15   14

Fear Street is a registered trademark of Parachute Press, Inc.

AN ARCHWAY PAPERBACK and colophon are registered trademarks of Simon & Schuster Inc.

Cover illustration by Bill Schmidt

Printed in the U.S.A.

IL 6+

The Stepsister

chapter
1

"*I* hate my hair!"

Emily Casey made an exasperated face at herself in the mirror and tossed her hairbrush across the room.

"You're just freaked out because Jessie and Rich are coming," Nancy said, lying on her stomach on the bed, an old copy of *Sassy* magazine in front of her.

"No. I hate my hair!" Emily insisted. Scowling, she walked over to the bed and picked the hairbrush up from the carpet. "It looks like shredded wheat," she said, returning to the full-length mirror on the closet door and beginning to brush again.

"How do you know what shredded wheat looks like?" Nancy asked, not looking up from the magazine. "You don't eat shredded wheat. You don't eat anything."

"Then why am I so fat?" Emily wailed, pushing at the sides of her hair with her hand.

"You're not fat," Nancy said, flipping the pages.

1

"You're just not petite like Mom and me. You're big-boned. You're tall. You're—"

"Fat," Emily said glumly. She knew she wasn't really fat. She just felt like complaining. Maybe Nancy was right. Maybe she *was* just freaked out because her new stepsister and stepbrother were coming to stay. She hated it when Nancy was right.

"I hate it when you're right," she said aloud. "Why do you have to sound like such a big sister?"

"Next you'll complain about your hands," Nancy said, closing the magazine and tossing it to the floor.

"My hands?"

"How they're too big. That's what always comes next. First your hair, then your size, then your big, ugly hands."

Emily sighed. "My hair is just too fine. It won't fall. It won't bounce. It won't do anything. Stop making fun of me."

"What's a big sister for?"

"I don't know," Emily said dryly. She laughed.

"You look okay," Nancy said. "Where'd you get that short skirt? From my closet?"

"No. It's mine. I think." Emily adjusted it nervously, then pulled up the black tights she wore underneath it.

"Since when do you wear skirts?" Nancy asked, pulling herself up to a sitting position on the edge of the bed.

"I wanted to dress up. You know. Make a good impression."

"You really *are* nervous," Nancy said with a smug smile. She stood up and walked over to the mirror.

She was wearing designer jeans that emphasized her slight, boyish figure, and a pale green turtleneck sweater that looked sensational against her copper-red hair. Unlike Emily's, Nancy's hair was straight and smooth and always fell right into place at the touch of a comb.

"Mom baked a cake," Emily said. "Guess she's nervous too."

"It'll probably taste like cement."

Standing side by side, the girls didn't look at all like sisters. "How come you're so cool?" Emily asked, picking the magazine up from the floor and placing it on the shelf with the others. "Don't you think it's exciting that we're going to have a new sister and brother?"

"We've met them before," Nancy said, walking over to the bedroom window and staring down at the front lawn that sloped gently down to Fear Street. It was a sunny day, warm for December. Spindly shadows of the barren trees played against the patterned yellow wallpaper.

"So what?" Emily cried heatedly. "They're coming to *live* with us. I mean, *forever.*"

"I'm going away to college next year," Nancy said. "Besides, Jessie is going to be in your room. You're the one who has to make the sacrifices."

Emily stared at her sister, a little startled by Nancy's words. Emily had been so excited that she was getting a new sister her own age, she had never thought of it as a sacrifice.

Maybe it *was* a sacrifice. Maybe giving up her privacy, giving up half her space, was a big sacrifice.

She had met Jessie several times, and they'd always gotten along fine. But that wasn't the same as having Jessie actually living with her. What if she turned out to be a real dweeb?

No. That's stupid, she quickly decided. Nancy was so negative. She wasn't going to let Nancy make her more nervous than she already was.

"Getting a stepfather, that was the *big* change," Nancy said, staring hard out the window, as if trying to avoid looking at Emily.

Nancy never wanted to talk about Hugh Wallner, the man their mother had married three months before. Emily knew that Nancy didn't really like him. Emily didn't like him that much either. He was so different from their father. Both girls had to decide whether to keep their old last name or change to his, and both had decided to keep their old name. That must have hurt their new stepfather, just a little. But he was a stern, private man for the most part, and he didn't let on.

As long as Mom is happy, it's okay, Emily thought. And her mother seemed blissfully happy being Mrs. Hugh Wallner.

Emily sat down on the new bed near the window, the bed that would be Jessie's. She smoothed out the red and blue patterned bedspread. The mattress felt so hard and new. "Jessie's great," she said. "She and I had a great time at Mom's wedding."

"She's very pretty, in a way," Nancy said. She never liked to give completely positive compliments.

Suddenly there was a rapid thumping sound out in the hall. Tiger, Emily's small white terrier, came bounding into the room, full speed as always, yipping and breathing noisily. "Stay down, Tiger!" Emily yelled.

But she wasn't fast enough. The little dog leapt up into her lap, stood on his hind legs, and reached up to lick her face.

"No—my hair! Don't mess up my hair!"

But those were words the dog didn't understand. By the time Emily managed to pull Tiger off her, her hair on the left side was standing straight out. "Oh, Tiger, I love you!" Emily held him up to her face and rubbed noses with him. "Even if you do destroy my hair!" She let him down. Tiger, his stub of a tail flicking furiously back and forth, toddled rapidly from the room and down the stairs.

"Hey—they're here!" Nancy cried, turning away from the window. "What happened to your hair?"

"Tell them I'll be down in a minute," Emily said with a sigh, rummaging on her dresser top for the hairbrush.

"It *does* look like shredded wheat," Nancy said, heading to the stairs. "Maybe you should wear a hat."

"Thanks for the support, Nance."

"Just trying to be helpful." Nancy disappeared.

"Now, do come in. Do come in." Emily could hear her mother at the front door, welcoming Jessie and Rich in an excited voice. "You both look wonderful. We're all so excited. Where's Emily?"

"The plane was late, as usual," Mr. Wallner grumbled.

"Well, they're here now. And that's all that counts," Emily's mother said. Emily stood at the top of the stairs, her heart pounding, listening to the excited voices. This is going to work out fine, she thought. In fact, it's really going to be *fun*.

She took a deep breath and hurried down the stairs, taking them two at a time. "Hi!" She rushed forward to hug Jessie, who was in the middle of taking off her plum-colored down coat. Emily, somewhat flustered, hugged the coat instead.

Both girls laughed.

"Well, hi, anyway," Emily said. "You look great!"

Jessie was a very pretty girl. Everything about her was tiny and petite, except for her eyes, which were startlingly large and pale blue. She had long, crimped straw-blond hair, a beautiful, high forehead, and creamy white skin. She reminded Emily of old paintings of angels she had seen in a museum. Jessie was wearing a pale blue sweater, obviously chosen because it matched her eyes and her faded jeans.

"Thanks," she said to Emily, handing her coat to her father. "You look great too." She had a soft, whispery voice that perfectly matched her looks. Her eyes went to Emily's hair and lingered there awhile. Then she turned to Mrs. Wallner. "It feels so great to be here," she gushed. "I just love this house!" She rushed forward and gave Mrs. Wallner a long hug. Emily saw that her mother was genuinely moved by this.

"Hey—let's not forget Rich," Nancy chimed in, interrupting Jessie's hug.

"Well, of course we won't forget Rich," Mrs. Wallner said, beaming at him. "How could I forget such a handsome young man? Even if he is the strong silent type." Mrs. Wallner winked, obviously pleased with her little joke.

Rich, normally as pale as his sister, turned tomato red.

"Well, *someone's* got to be quiet around here," Nancy cracked.

Everyone laughed except Rich, who still looked very embarrassed by all the attention. He was thin and wiry. He seemed too tall for his body. He was blond like his sister, with short, spiky hair. He had a few pimples sprinkled on his chin. And he had enormous feet. With the white sneakers he wore, he looked just like a cartoon rabbit!

Thirteen-year-olds are so weird, Emily thought. She couldn't remember being thirteen even though it was only three years ago. She had forced all memories of it from her mind.

"What's that you're reading?" Emily asked him.

He had a hardcover book in his hand. He started to raise it to show her.

"That boy always has a book with him," Mr. Wallner said, shaking his head, as if disapproving.

"It—it's Stephen King," Rich muttered, so low Emily could barely hear him.

"Pet Sematary. You read that one, didn't you, Nancy?" Emily asked.

Nancy turned up her nose. "'I don't read Stephen King anymore."

"Now that she's a senior, she doesn't read anything!" Emily cracked to Jessie.

Jessie laughed appreciatively, even though it wasn't much of a joke.

"It's just so good to be here. I know we're going to be very happy," Jessie said to Mrs. Wallner in her breathy voice.

"I'm sure we all will," Mrs. Wallner replied.

"It'll be so neat having a sister my age," Jessie said, turning to Emily. "We can study together and go everywhere together. You'll have to show me Shadyside. We can cook together. Do you like to cook? And we can share each other's clothes and—"

"I don't think we can do that," Emily said, suddenly embarrassed. Jessie was so much smaller than she.

"It's just going to be the *best*," Jessie gushed, and rushed forward to give Emily a hug.

"I baked a cake," Mrs. Wallner said, "and I've got sandwiches all ready. I knew you'd be hungry after your flight."

"I'm starving," Mr. Wallner said, holding his hands on top of his stomach. "Waiting around in airports gives me indigestion."

He was tall and muscular, balding with a fringe of dark hair around his head. To Emily, he always seemed disgruntled, unhappy about something, about to get indigestion.

"But before we eat, I'll bet Jessie and Rich would like to go upstairs and unpack and see their rooms," Mrs. Wallner said, ignoring her husband.

"That's a great idea," Jessie said, picking up her enormous suitcase.

"No, let me carry that for you," Emily said. She immediately regretted making the offer. She could barely lift the case off the ground.

"I'll bring the suitcases up later," Mr. Wallner said, heading toward the kitchen.

Nancy led Rich up to his room, the very narrow room that up until a few days before had been a storage closet at the end of the hall. "Come on, Jessie," Emily said brightly. "I'll show you our room."

"Great," Jessie said, smiling at Mrs. Wallner. "We'll be down in a few minutes. I'm starting to feel really hungry too."

"I'll get everything ready," Mrs. Wallner said happily, following her husband to the kitchen. "Hey, Hugh—don't eat up everything before the kids get a bite!"

Jessie followed Emily up the carpeted stairs, which creaked and shifted under their feet. "Ta-daa! Here it is," Emily said, ushering Jessie in.

Jessie frowned as her eyes quickly surveyed the room. "Kind of small," she muttered.

"Huh?" Emily wasn't sure she heard right. Jessie had such a whispery voice.

Still frowning, Jessie walked over to the open window and, leaning against the sill, looked out. "Fear Street. What a name."

"It's a very interesting neighborhood," Emily said.

"How long have you lived in this old dump?" Jessie asked, turning to Emily. It seemed more like an accusation than a question.

"Uh . . . about six years, I guess," Emily said, trying to think how old she was when they moved here. "My parents like old houses. I mean *liked*. My dad, he was really handy. He loved to fix things up."

"Is your mother always so cheerful and enthusiastic

9

like that?" Jessie asked, quickly changing the subject. She rolled her eyes. "I mean, wow." She stepped back from the window and sat down on Emily's bed, then lay back, supporting her head in her hands.

Uh-oh, Emily thought. Jessie is so different as soon as the adults are out of sight. She was so sweet downstairs. But now she has a whole new personality. Is this what she's *really* like?

"Mom was just excited," Emily said uncomfortably.

Jessie sat up and picked up Maxie, Emily's treasured old teddy bear. "You don't look like your mom," she said, looking Emily up and down.

She's staring at my big hands, Emily thought. She clasped her hands behind her back and walked over to the desk. "No. But my sister looks exactly like her. Exactly."

"I never liked red hair," Jessie said, making a face. She examined the old teddy bear, then looked back up at Emily. "There isn't much closet space in here, is there? What am I supposed to do with all my stuff?"

She must have caught the wary look on Emily's face, because she immediately started to apologize. "I'm really sorry. Please. Forget everything I've said up here. I—I'm just so nervous."

"I'm nervous too," Emily admitted. "You really don't have to apologize."

"Yes, I do. I was just being stupid. This—it's all been so hard. I mean, it's been terrible."

Emily turned the desk chair around to face Jessie and sat down in it. "What do you mean?"

"I mean, as soon as Mom found out that Daddy was

getting remarried, she couldn't wait to shove Rich and me off on him. It's not too cool to find out your own mother doesn't want you around."

"I'm sorry," Emily said softly.

"Rich and I have been like yo-yos," Jessie said bitterly, staring down at the carpet. "It's like we've been shuttled back and forth between the two of them our whole lives." She tossed the teddy bear from hand to hand. "Also, I had to leave everyone. All my friends. My best friend, Debra. Debra and I—we were really close. I miss her already."

"I'm really sorry," Emily repeated. "I didn't really understand how hard this is for you."

"Well, it's tough," Jessie said, still unable to look at Emily.

"I'll try my best to—" Emily started. But she was interrupted by the familiar tiny thunder of dog paws. Tiger burst into the room, leapt up onto the bed, and tried to lick Jessie's face.

"Ugh! Get away!" Jessie screamed, shoving Tiger away. "Get off me!" She shoved him hard. The confused terrier let out a confused yelp as he hit the floor. "That awful dog will get hair all over my new sweater!" Jessie wailed. "Get him out of here!"

"Tiger—out," Emily said firmly.

The dog didn't have to be told twice. His stub of a tail straight up in the air, he turned and trotted out.

"He's really very sweet," Emily said, annoyed at Jessie's violent reaction to Tiger.

"He's disgusting," Jessie said, searching her sweater for dog hairs.

"He doesn't shed much at all," Emily told her.

"He could've torn it," Jessie whined. "Do you know what this sweater cost?"

"It's very pretty," Emily said, a little embarrassed. To change the subject she asked, "Are you starving now? You want to go back downstairs?"

"Yeah. I guess." Jessie moved Emily's old teddy bear from hand to hand.

"I was given that bear on my first birthday," Emily told her. "It was always my favorite."

"Really?" Jessie pinched the bear's nose. "It's pretty tacky now, isn't it?" She laughed, a whispery, high-pitched laugh.

"It means a lot to me," Emily replied.

"Guess I'll take this bed, Emily. I can't stand sleeping by a window."

"But that's always been *my* bed," Emily protested. "We bought that new bed by the window for you."

"Well . . . then I think we have a problem."

Jessie glared unhappily at Emily. Then she looked down and tore the head off the teddy bear.

chapter

2

The Last Camp-out

Jessie laughed a startled, high-pitched laugh.

Emily was still too shocked to say a word. Was this really happening?

Jessie quickly choked off her laughter. "I'm so sorry," she said, looking down at the teddy bear head in her left hand and the body in her right hand, gray stuffing falling through the open neck. "It was an accident. Really." She looked up at Emily, as if to see if Emily believed her.

Emily didn't believe her. "You pulled Max's head off," she said. For some reason it came out more like a question than an accusation.

"No. It just came off in my hands," Jessie insisted. "Really. I barely touched it. You do believe me, don't you?" Her large blue eyes burned into Emily's, as if challenging Emily to agree it was an accident.

Emily didn't reply.

A shadow fell across the room. It was caused by clouds covering the sun outside the bedroom window. The room darkened so suddenly it gave Emily an eerie feeling. She had this strange sensation that Jessie had brought on the darkness. Emily shivered, suddenly chilled.

It was a silly thought, of course. But the picture of Jessie in the darkened room sitting on Emily's bed with Max torn in half on her lap would stay with Emily for a long, long time.

The shadow lifted.

"Hey, guys." Nancy walked into the room. She was carrying a handful of cassettes. "How's it going? Do you want these back, Em? I borrowed them last week and—"

She stopped in midsentence. "Hey—what happened to Max?"

"It was an accident. Really!" Jessie cried, sounding very defensive. She stood up quickly and walked over to Nancy, holding up the two teddy bear parts. "It just came off in my hands." Jessie's voice trembled.

Nancy put the cassettes down on the desk and took the teddy bear from Jessie. "Maybe it can be sewn," she said. She looked at Emily.

"Maybe," Emily said doubtfully.

"Hey, your brother sure is quiet," Nancy said to Jessie, deliberately changing the subject. She handed the teddy bear to Emily.

"Tell me about it," Jessie said dryly. "Rich is quiet, okay? But once you get to know him, he's just about silent!"

Nancy laughed. Jessie laughed at her own joke. Emily still didn't feel like laughing.

Jessie has a real mean streak, she thought. She's only been here a few minutes, and she's already putting down her brother.

Then she realized that maybe she was being ridiculous. Jessie had just made a joke, after all. And maybe the teddy bear thing *was* an accident. Max had been practically falling apart for years. Here Emily was, thinking the worst about Jessie when she should have been trying to make her feel at home, feel like part of the family.

She *is* part of the family now, Emily told herself. You've *got* to get along with Jessie.

"It must be hard for Rich," Emily said sympathetically. "Starting all over in a new school is rough."

"Tell me about it," Jessie said with some bitterness. Then she laughed, a nervous laugh. "Rich is okay, I guess. He and I really don't talk much. It's hard to get close to him. He's sort of in his own world. Always walking around with some creepy book in his hand. He must be the biggest Stephen King fan in the world. He even writes him letters."

The room darkened again. The sky outside the window was completely gray now. The colors in the room all seemed to fade into shades of gray.

"I never liked Stephen King all that much," Nancy said. "Of course now that I'm a senior, I don't have time to read *anything*. Just schoolwork. And college applications, of course."

"Are you going out tonight?" Emily asked quickly.

15

She didn't want Nancy to get started on how hard it was being a senior and how much work she had to do. Nancy could talk for hours on that subject. It sometimes seemed to Emily that Nancy spent more time talking about how hard the work was than doing the work. And when she wasn't complaining about all the homework, she was complaining about her social life. "Don't you have a date with Gary Brandt?"

"He called and broke the date," Nancy said, shaking her head. "Said he had a cold. But he didn't even have the decency to sniffle once or twice into the phone. I knew he wouldn't show." She picked up the cassettes and then let them drop one by one back onto the desk. "Let's not bore Jessie with the details of my social life," she said with a forced laugh. "It's been such a mess ever since—"

"I know, I know," Emily groaned, rolling her eyes. "Ever since Josh broke up with you and started going out with me."

Jessie climbed to her feet, looking very uncomfortable. "Maybe I should go downstairs," she said, looking first at Emily, then at Nancy. "If you two want to tear each other's eyes out or something . . ."

"No, no," Emily said, jumping up too. "Nancy and I have been over this a thousand times."

"Two thousand," Nancy said, brushing her copper hair back over her shoulder.

She looks just like Mom when she does that, Emily thought.

"Nancy, you know you couldn't stand the sight of Josh anymore," Emily said, wondering why she was bothering to defend herself again. "You told me you were going to break up with him, remember?"

Nancy flushed. She seemed embarrassed to be discussing this in front of Jessie. "You're right. You're totally right, Em. In fact, I really don't know what you see in him. He's such a creep!" She laughed, trying to make it all sound like a joke. She turned to Jessie. "Josh's idea of dressing up for a date is to turn his sweatshirt around so the dirty part is in back!"

"Hey, that's not fair!" Emily cried.

Jessie and Nancy laughed.

Why is she going into all this now? Emily wondered. Josh doesn't mean anything to Nancy. She's told me a million times that she doesn't care that I'm dating him now.

"I'm hungry. I'm going downstairs," Nancy said, heading for the door. "You coming?"

"Be down in a second," Emily said, setting the two parts of the teddy bear down on the desk.

"I like your sister," Jessie said as soon as Nancy had gone downstairs. "She's so pretty. Are you really dating her old boyfriend?"

"They didn't go together that long," Emily said brusquely. She really wanted to drop the subject.

"So, are we agreed?" Jessie asked. "I get the bed by the wall?"

"Well . . ." It isn't settled at all, Emily thought crossly. That's *my* bed!

"And can we move that night-table over to my side?" Jessie asked. Without waiting for a reply, she began tugging the night-table across the room.

"I'll have to empty it out for you," Emily said quietly. Is Jessie trying to bully me? she wondered. Is she always going to have to get her way? Is she going to boss me around in my own house?

It's her house too, Emily reminded herself. It's her house too—from now on. . . .

"Well, this is a real party!" Mrs. Wallner said, beaming happily from the head of the dining-room table. Mr. Wallner muttered agreement, a pleased smile on his usually dour face.

Emily and Nancy had decorated the dining room, stringing crepe-paper streamers over the doorway and over the dark green wallpaper above the buffet, and hanging big cut-out letters spelling WELCOME over the double windows. Their mom had put a white linen tablecloth on the table, a special departure from the straw place mats they usually used. Two dozen pink and red roses in a big cut-glass vase served as a beautiful centerpiece. Emily couldn't remember the old house ever looking this festive.

"How about a toast?" she said, pouring some Coke into her glass, trying to forget about the unpleasantness upstairs and get into a party mood. She passed the big Coke bottle to Jessie.

"Do you have any diet soda?" Jessie asked Mrs. Wallner. "This is just too fattening."

Mrs. Wallner gave Jessie a look of surprise. "Don't tell me you worry about your weight, Jessie. If you got any skinnier, we wouldn't be able to see you!"

Mr. Wallner laughed loudly. "Jessie worries about

everything," he said, shaking his head. He turned to Rich at the end of the table. Rich hadn't said a word. "How ya doin', pal?" Mr. Wallner called down to him.

"Okay," Rich said with a shrug.

"Why don't you put that book down and have some cake," Mr. Wallner suggested.

"Okay," Rich said, closing his book.

"Do you want ice cream with your cake?" Emily's mom asked.

Rich muttered something.

"Speak up, Rich. Your words are falling right into your lap," Mr. Wallner said.

"Yes. Ice cream, please," Rich replied, louder. His voice cracked on the word *please*.

Mr. Wallner laughed at him. "You sound like a boy soprano!" he said.

Rich turned bright red and lowered his eyes.

"Stop picking on him, Daddy," Jessie said sharply.

"I'm not picking on him. I just made a joke," Mr. Wallner said, stuffing a big forkful of the vanilla cake into his mouth and washing it down with a long swallow of coffee from his cup.

"Some joke," Rich muttered, still not raising his eyes.

"What did you say? Are you muttering again?"

"Give him a break, Daddy," Jessie insisted shrilly.

Rich pushed his chair back with a loud squeal and stood up awkwardly. "Can I just go upstairs and read?" He didn't wait for an answer. He picked up the Stephen King book and, without looking at any of them, hurried out of the room.

"Hey—what did *I* do?" Mr. Wallner asked, throwing up his hands, suddenly sounding very childish.

"You're always embarrassing him, Daddy," Jessie said, frowning.

"I didn't mean to," he replied with a mouthful of cake. "I'll go upstairs and apologize after I finish my cake. This *is* supposed to be a party, after all."

"Should he be reading a book like that?" Emily's mom asked, sounding concerned. *"Pet Sematary* is supposed to be pretty gruesome, isn't it?"

"He loves Stephen King," Jessie told her.

"He's a real bookworm," Mr. Wallner said, pouring more coffee into his cup. "Not like his old dad. I don't think I've picked up a book since high school."

Emily glanced over at Nancy, who returned her look. Both girls were thinking the same thing: That's nothing to brag about. Both girls were also thinking how different Mr. Wallner was from their father.

Emily looked at him, sitting at the table in his oversize, yellow sleeveless T-shirt and baggy, brown slacks with their attached elastic belt, and thought of how well dressed her father had always been. Dan Casey had been a pediatrician. He had always worn dark, serious suits with starched white shirts and conservative ties. He had been very young-looking—he had barely looked older than his twenties—and dressed to make himself look older so that the parents who brought their children to him would feel more confident.

Her father, Emily remembered, had read two or three books a week, books of all kinds, which he liked to discuss with his two daughters. He would never have bragged about not having picked up a book in years.

How could Mom have married someone so different from Daddy? Emily asked herself. Mr. Wallner was a manager in a furniture factory. He didn't even wear a tie to work!

Mom had been so lonely, Emily thought. Maybe she just settled.

She tried not to think about that terrible day on the lake. But she couldn't keep the memories away. It was as if they had a life of their own. Emily could be in school, taking an exam, or at a movie, or on a date, or sitting at the dining-room table as she was now, and the memories would flood back to her, forcing her to relive the horror again . . . and again.

Her dad had loved to camp out. The whole family did. Sometimes they wouldn't even wait for the warm weather to come. They'd load the station wagon with equipment and drive off to a state park or a nearby forest area and spend the weekend roughing it in the bright blue canvas tents Mr. Casey kept in the garage.

That weekend they'd been camping on Fear Island, the small, uninhabited, wooded island in the center of the lake across from the Fear Street woods. The weather was exhilaratingly brisk, to say the least. A strong gusting wind made the normally calm lake waters toss and tumble into white, frothy waves.

The tents flapped noisily in the wind. It was hard to get the campfire lit, and once lit the flames darted out in all directions, pushed by the shifting winds.

The air smelled so piney and fresh. Even Nancy, who had to be dragged along because she had to cancel a date with Josh, was cheered by the beauty of the woods, the excitement of being the only people for miles around.

Why had Emily and her father been in the power-boat?

Her memories of that terrible day were so vivid. But for some reason she couldn't remember getting into the boat, couldn't remember where they were headed, why they had decided to battle the choppy, wind-tossed waters.

Maybe that was the reason. Maybe Emily and her dad had just wanted to challenge the wind, challenge the rolling, dark waves. Maybe they had done it for the excitement. It wouldn't have been the first time.

She remembered Nancy and her mom waving to them from the wooded shore. She remembered them as tiny, light figures against the dark, bending trees. She remembered the roar of the small outboard motor, the bobbing of the boat, the funny weak feeling in her knees. And she remembered how cold it was, the wet spray on her face, her dark hair so wet, flying back against her shoulders, flying in the wind.

She turned to see her father, who smiled at her, his hand on the control. Drops of water trickled down the front of his blue down vest. She could see them so clearly. The outboard motor roared. The little boat seemed to fly over the tumultuous waters. It was such a wonderful feeling. The two of them were enjoying it so much.

It all turned to horror so quickly.

Emily was handing the thermos to her dad. The hot

coffee had tasted delicious. Her hand was wet. The thermos slid away from her, into the water.

Without thinking, her dad reached for it.

The wind came up, such a strong, sudden wind.

It felt as if the world were turning upside down.

It took a few seconds for Emily to realize that the boat was capsizing.

The frozen water didn't make it any more real. It was all like a dream, a strange, frightening dream.

She remembered thinking, This can't really be happening.

She went under. Forcing herself back up to the surface gave her time to realize what was happening.

"Daddy! Daddy—where are you?"

A wave slapped her hard. She started to choke.

The overturned boat bobbed a few yards away. She swam for it, was pushed back, swam harder, still sputtering.

"Daddy—where are you?"

She grabbed the boat. It was so slippery, but somehow she managed to hold on. Another gust of wind sent the waters high. She gripped the boat bottom with both hands.

"Daddy! Daddy!"

Where was he?

She turned and looked behind her. She looked all around.

Was he swimming back toward the island?

It was a low, dark line against the gray sky.

"Daddy? Where are you, Daddy?"

He wouldn't swim away and leave her.

The island was too far to swim to, especially against the current.

Where was he?

She remembered the panic. It filled her chest, made it hard to breathe.

The panic spread over her entire body, froze her there, clinging hard to the overturned boat.

It seemed like hours.

It must have been only seconds.

And then she saw him.

He floated slowly past her, face down, his light brown hair floating on the surface of the water like seaweed.

chapter
3

Gone Forever

"**I**'ve got to get off the phone, Josh. Mom's calling me down for dinner." Emily twisted her fingers in the white phone cord. She had been lying on her back on the bed, staring up at the ceiling, but now she pulled herself up and prepared to hang up the phone.

"Yeah. Okay. Come over later," she said, hearing water running in the bathroom and figuring it must be Jessie. "But give me time to finish writing my report. I've got about another hour to go on it."

Josh had already finished the paper he was working on, of course. Mister Super-Speed. If he didn't finish an assignment two or three days early, he thought he was slipping. It drove Emily crazy. She was a hard worker, but she always had to work right down to the last minute.

"Yeah, it's going pretty well with Jessie," she said, lowering her voice. "I really can't talk now. She's right across the hall in the bathroom. Yeah. Yeah. We haven't really talked much. She's been so busy getting used to a new school and everything. She's still real tense. I don't know if it's me or what."

"It's definitely you," Josh said, and then laughed, his silly, high-pitched laugh.

"Maybe she's just a tense person," Emily said, ignoring his joke. "Well, see you later. Come after nine, okay?"

She stood up and replaced the receiver, tried to straighten her hair, frowning into the full-length mirror on the closet door, and then hurried downstairs to the dining room. Jessie has barely said five words to me in the three days she's been here, she thought. Emily couldn't help but feel disappointed. She had looked forward to having a new sister. But so far she and Jessie were just two strangers who happened to share a room.

"Sorry, I'm late," she said, scooting into her place. Mr. Wallner was already half finished with his plate of macaroni. He always sat down and started to eat whether anyone was at the table or not.

Across from him Nancy yawned loudly. "Sorry," she said, shaking her head. "I was up studying till nearly two last night."

"You really are working hard this year," Mrs. Wallner said, passing the bowl of macaroni to Emily.

"You should get your beauty sleep," Mr. Wallner said. It must have been meant as a joke, because he stopped chewing for a moment to laugh. He looked disappointed that no one else at the table saw the humor of it. "Pass the salt and pepper," he muttered.

"Is it too bland?" Mrs. Wallner asked.

"No. It's fine," he replied, using both hands to cover his food with salt and pepper at the same time.

Rich, silent as usual, sat staring into his plate, occasionally lifting a macaroni noodle or two to his mouth.

"Where's Jessie?" Nancy asked.

"I think she's upstairs in the bathroom," Emily said, reaching for the salad bowl.

"Did you brush your hair today?" Mrs. Wallner asked, making a disapproving face at Emily.

"I have to wash it tonight," Emily said, annoyed. Her mother knew she didn't like to talk about her hair.

"Come on, Rich. Dig into that macaroni," Mr. Wallner said, pouring more pepper on his. "It's delicious."

"I'm not very hungry," Rich said sullenly.

"You're never hungry," Mr. Wallner grumbled. "That's why you *look* like a macaroni noodle."

"Hey, why are you always putting me down?" Rich shouted, immediately angry.

"I wasn't putting you down. That was a compliment," Mr. Wallner said, smiling at Rich.

"You can shove your compliments!" Rich cried, angrily tossing his fork down onto his plate and storming out of the room.

"Hey, come back here," Mr. Wallner called after him, startled and obviously upset. "I was just teasing you!" He turned to Emily's mother. "What's with that kid?"

"Thirteen is a really hard age," Mrs. Wallner said, suddenly looking very tired.

"I'll make it a lot *harder* for him," Mr. Wallner said. But it wasn't a threat. Everyone could see that he was very upset by Rich's angry reaction. He reached for the salad bowl and piled a heap of lettuce on his plate. "I'm getting sick and tired of him running away anytime anybody says anything to him."

"He's very sensitive," Mrs. Wallner said softly.

"Don't defend him."

"I wasn't defending him. I was just explaining—"

"Well, don't explain either." Mr. Wallner angrily forked lettuce into his mouth.

"Sorry I'm late. I got hung up," Jessie said, hurrying into the room. Her blond hair sparkled under the dining-room lights. She was wearing gray wool slacks and a long, pale green sweater.

"Hey—my sweater!" Emily cried.

"What?" Jessie scooted her chair in and gave Emily a confused look.

"That's my sweater. You're wearing my sweater," Emily insisted, sounding angrier than she had intended.

"No, it isn't," Jessie said, spooning a small helping of macaroni onto her plate.

"I'm afraid it must be cold by now," Mrs. Wallner said, frowning.

"Jessie, that sweater was in my top drawer," Emily said, unable to keep the shrillness from her voice. "I really wish you wouldn't borrow my stuff without asking."

"But it's *my* sweater," Jessie insisted.

28

"I know my own sweater," Emily said, feeling herself lose her temper, knowing she was getting out of control but unable to do anything about it. "Look how big it is on you. The shoulders are almost down to your elbows!"

"They're supposed to be. It's an oversize sweater," Jessie said huffily.

"Girls, please—" Mr. Wallner said, wearily resting his balding head on one hand.

"Mom, would you please tell Jessie not to wear my sweaters," Emily pleaded.

Mrs. Wallner looked at Emily, then at Jessie. "I really don't remember that sweater, Em," she said uncertainly. "Maybe it just looks like yours."

"Aaggggh!" Her mom's reply really infuriated Emily. Why was she taking Jessie's side?

"It's *not* your sweater," Jessie insisted heatedly. "I've had it for years."

"Listen," Mr. Wallner said, rubbing his eyes. He turned to Emily. "What difference does it make? You two are sisters now—right?"

"That's right," Emily's mother said quickly, *too* quickly, as far as Emily was concerned. "I'm sure there will be times when you'll want to borrow Jessie's clothes, Em."

"How *could* I?" Emily shrieked. "Look at her! She's five sizes smaller than I am!"

Mrs. Wallner's mouth dropped open. She always did that when she was surprised by something someone said. "Don't exaggerate, dear."

"Let's finish our dinner in peace," said Nancy, who had been watching the entire argument in silence.

"Then we'll go upstairs and do a fingerprint test on your dresser, okay?"

For some reason Mr. Wallner found this very funny. He laughed, scratching his bald head.

Obviously this was the end of the discussion. Emily didn't feel much like eating, but she grudgingly began forking cold macaroni and cheese into her mouth. She knew Jessie was looking at her, but she refused to return her glance.

"Nancy, do you have a date Saturday night?" Mrs. Wallner asked, changing the subject. "Mrs. Bergen called and asked if you were free to baby-sit."

"Yeah. I don't have a date," Nancy said, sighing. "I'll call her later."

"Glad someone's earning a little money around here," Mr. Wallner muttered, looking at Jessie. She didn't respond. They finished their dinner in silence.

"Who's going to clean up?" Mrs. Wallner asked. "Now, don't everybody volunteer at once."

Mr. Wallner grinned. "Not me. That's what I like about living with four women. There's always someone to clean up after dinner."

"You're a sexist pig," Mrs. Wallner said. But she said it with a smile, and she walked up behind her husband and kissed him loudly on the forehead.

She's totally crazy about him, Emily thought with some dismay. What on *earth* does she see in him? He really *is* a sexist pig!

"It's Emily's turn," Jessie said. "Nancy and I cleaned up last night."

"Can you take my turn tonight?" Emily asked, staring at her sweater on Jessie. "I've just got to get up to the computer and finish my social studies report. I'll clean up three nights in a row. I promise."

Jessie reluctantly agreed. Emily excused herself and started to leave the room. "How's the report going?" Mr. Wallner asked. "It's on Chile, right?"

Emily was a bit stunned that her new stepfather remembered what she was working on. She didn't think he was at all interested in her schoolwork. "I've written pages and pages," she told him. "I just have to finish writing the last part and then print it out."

"Could I see it after you print it out?" he asked.

"Sure. Okay. Great," Emily stammered.

It was the first time he had really tried to reach out to her, and she was surprised to see that she felt really pleased.

She hurried up to her room, sat down at the desk, and clicked on the computer. She slid in her disk, then remembered her sweater. She turned and looked over at her dresser. Was the top drawer slightly open? She couldn't really tell. Besides, what would that prove?

Should she get up and look for it? No. She had to get the report on Chile finished and printed out before Josh arrived. *Yes.* She was too curious not to look.

She walked over to the dresser and pulled open the drawer. The sweater, she remembered clearly, had been right on top. It wasn't there now. She searched through the drawer quickly. No sweater.

Jessie had been lying. Jessie was wearing her sweater.

"I can't think about this now," she told herself, pushing the dresser drawer back in and walking back to the desk.

She called up her report on the computer and then searched her trapper-keeper for her notes. She had already written twelve pages. Just two more sections to write. She found her place and began to type, her fingers clicking rapidly over the keyboard.

Down the hall she could hear the blare of heavy metal music filtering through Rich's closed bedroom door. From downstairs she could hear the clatter of dishes. Concentrating harder, she shut out all of the sounds and worked on transferring her notes onto the computer in sentences that resembled English.

She worked nonstop for nearly forty-five minutes, then realized that she was starving. Because of the dispute over the sweater, she hadn't eaten much dinner. She scrolled back the last two paragraphs she had written and read them over, leaning forward until her face was just inches from the amber monitor screen.

Pleased with what she had done so far, Emily took a deep breath, stretched, and headed down to the kitchen for a snack. "Hey, where is everyone?" she called, startled to find the dinner dishes all cleaned, everything back in place, and no one around.

She took an apple from the fruit bin in the refrigerator, washed it off at the kitchen sink, and took a bite. It was crunchy and fairly sweet. Hearing sounds in the den, she walked over to the doorway. Her mom and stepfather were on the brown leather couch. Making out like teenagers.

Emily tiptoed back to the hallway, then climbed the stairs to her room.

"Hey!" she cried out.

Jessie, seated at the computer, looked up slowly. "Oh, hi."

"What are you doing there?" Emily cried. "I'm working on my report."

Jessie's tiny features narrowed in confusion. "Oh. I'm sorry. I thought you were finished." She pushed the desk chair back and climbed to her feet. "It's all yours," she said, gesturing grandly to the computer with a sweep of her hands. "Let me know when you're finished, okay?"

"Yeah. Sure," Emily said. She sat down at the keyboard and called up her report.

But it didn't come up on the screen.

Feeling her throat tighten with apprehension, she called up the report again.

START A NEW FILE? the screen asked.

She checked the list of files.

And uttered a silent cry when the report did not appear there.

Emily stared at the screen in disbelief. She realized her hands were trembling.

Her report had been erased. It was gone. Gone forever.

"Jessie—" she screamed. "You erased my whole report!"

"What?" Jessie's pale blue eyes opened wide in surprise.

"You heard me!" Emily shrieked. "How *could* you?! You deliberately erased my whole report!" Emily was screaming at the top of her lungs, but she didn't care.

All of those days and days of work. Gone forever. This was the worst thing anyone had ever done to her.

"You erased *everything!*"

"I did not!" Jessie cried, backing away from Emily. "The computer was turned off when I came into the room!"

"You filthy liar!"

Unable to contain her anger, Emily lunged at Jessie. She caught her by surprise, pushed her to the floor, jumped on top of her, and began pounding her with her fists in a rage that frightened even her.

chapter
4

"I Could Kill Her!"

"What on *earth*—!"

Mrs. Wallner was in the room first, followed by her grim-faced husband.

Emily had already stopped fighting. She gave no resistance as Mr. Wallner pulled her off Jessie. She stood up unsteadily, jerking out of his grip, shaking all over, surprised to find that her face was wet with tears.

When did I start to cry? she wondered.

"Jessie—what happened? Are you okay?" Mrs. Wallner leaned down and gently helped Jessie to her feet. Jessie's normally perfect hair was wet and matted against her face. She was breathing hard, gasping for breath, unable to speak.

"Oh, no! I tore the sweater!" Emily wailed, seeing the long rip on Jessie's sleeve.

"Is *that* what this is about? The sweater?" Mr. Wallner asked, his hands on his hips. He was forcing himself not to shout, to stay calm, but the veins on his temples throbbed, and his face was very red.

"What's going on?" Nancy and Rich pushed through the doorway into the bedroom at the same time.

"Nothing," Mr. Wallner said quickly. "You two—out." He pointed to the door. They stared at Jessie and Emily for a long moment, then obediently backed out of the room.

I've never been in a fight in my life, Emily thought. How did this happen? She grabbed up a handful of tissues from the box on her dresser and wiped her eyes and wet cheeks.

If only I could stop shaking.

"What is this about?" Mr. Wallner demanded.

"Ask her," Jessie said bitterly, fingering the tear in the sweater sleeve.

"Jessie deliberately erased my report," Emily said, her voice as shaky as the rest of her.

"That's a lie," Jessie said. "A total lie."

"I went downstairs for a snack," Emily started. "When I came back, Jessie was working on the computer, and my report—it was erased."

"Oh, how awful," Mrs. Wallner said sympathetically, shaking her head. "You've been working so hard on it. But, Emily, I'm sure it was an accident."

"Accident?!" Emily shrieked.

"Now, calm down, Emily. You're upset so you're not thinking clearly," her mother said.

"It's clear she did it on purpose!" Emily cried.

"Emily! Don't say things like that!" her mother raised her voice. "No matter what happened. There's no excuse for fighting. I can't believe you attacked Jessie."

"I attacked *her!*" Emily shrieked, her voice so high and shrill, it hurt her throat. "I wasn't the one who—"

"Stop. Just stop," her mother said, balling her hands into tight fists at her side. "I don't want to hear any more. I just know we can't have this kind of fighting in our house." She looked to her husband for support.

He nodded somberly but didn't say anything.

"But my whole report—!" Emily wailed.

"You two have *got* to work out your differences," Mr. Wallner said. "You have no choice. You *have* to get along."

"This must never happen again," Mrs. Wallner said.

"But don't you want to know what happened?" Emily cried, more a desperate plea than a question.

"We don't want to hear another word until you've apologized to Jessie," Mrs. Wallner said through clenched teeth.

Emily uttered a cry of protest. "Me? Apologize to *her?*"

"Yes," her mother insisted. "You jumped on her. You hit her. You tore her sweater . . . didn't you?"

"*Her* sweater?!"

"Emily . . ." Her mother's eyes narrowed in anger. She was about to explode, Emily realized. And if she exploded, the first thing she'd say was that Emily was grounded and couldn't see Josh for a week, or a month, or a year.

Emily sighed, a sigh of defeat, of resignation.

"That doesn't sound like an apology," her mother said.

"She doesn't have to apologize," Jessie said, rubbing her arm.

"That's very generous of you, Jessie," Mrs. Wallner said. "But *I* said she does."

"Sorry," Emily muttered to the floor.

"Frankly, I'm ashamed of both of you," Mr. Wallner said, shaking his head sadly. "This has made me very unhappy." He strode quickly out of the room, his hands stuffed into his pants pockets.

"I *know* you two can get along," Mrs. Wallner said, whispering for some reason after her husband left the room. "Just try harder—okay?"

Both girls muttered okay.

Mrs. Wallner stooped to pick up some notebook paper that had fallen from the desk, then walked out without looking at either of them.

I can't *believe* she was on Jessie's side, Emily thought, feeling completely betrayed.

She looked up to see Jessie, leaning against the closet door, glaring at her, her face tight, her normally placid eyes burning into Emily's.

"Don't ever do that again," Jessie said slowly, pronouncing each word distinctly, in a menacing, low voice Emily had never heard before.

Emily was so surprised, she just stared back at her.

"I don't know what you have against me," Jessie said bitterly. "I don't know why you're trying so hard to make me look bad. But I'm warning you, Emily—

just stop it. Don't ever embarrass me like that again in front of my father."

"You're warning *me?*" Emily started to protest. But Tiger scampered into the room, sniffed Emily's ankles, then, his tail stub wagging furiously, hurried over to do the same to Jessie.

"Get *out* of here, you filthy thing," Jessie snarled, and kicked at the little dog. Tiger yelped, more out of surprise than pain, and ran back to Emily.

"Don't kick my dog!" Emily shouted, feeling her anger begin to rise again.

"I didn't kick it," Jessie said. "I just kicked *at* it."

Emily picked Tiger up and hugged him. Carrying him against her shoulder, she turned and ran out of the room. She walked down the hall to Nancy's room. The door was open, so she walked in.

Nancy was sitting on her bed, a book in her lap, as if waiting for Emily. Nancy's room was smaller than Emily's, long and narrow, with a tall, pink-curtained window overlooking the backyard at the end. Nancy was a collector. She collected glass bottles, and shells, and interesting stones, and antique dolls, and old children's books, and charm-bracelet charms, and matchbooks, and baseball trading cards, among other things. To hold her collections, their father had built long wooden shelves that stretched along one entire wall of the room from floor to ceiling.

"Nancy has never thrown away or given away anything," he had always complained. "Someday we're going to have to give her the entire house just to hold her stuff."

Emily, who never seemed to be able to save or collect anything, really admired this quality in her sister. Sometimes she would wander into Nancy's room and just marvel at all of the things her sister had found interesting enough to save, running her hands over the smooth glass bottles, examining the tiny silver charms, even though she'd examined them at least a dozen times before.

Now she stopped in the doorway and put down Tiger, who immediately scampered away. "Can I come in?"

"Of course," Nancy said, putting aside her book. "Come sit down." She patted a spot beside her on the bedspread.

Emily gratefully sat down beside her sister. She stared down at the white shag rug at her feet, still feeling very shaky, and didn't say anything.

"You certainly look a mess," Nancy said with tenderness, not as a criticism.

Emily forced a faint smile. "I guess I do. But at least Jessie's hair got messed up. That's a first, right?"

"What on earth happened?" Nancy asked, running her hand through Emily's hair tenderly, pushing it back off her forehead. "Why were you fighting?"

"She erased my entire report," Emily said, sobbing despite her attempts to calm down.

"Do you think it was on purpose?"

"It *had* to be," Emily insisted. "All that work. Lost. Now I'll flunk social studies for sure."

"Emily, calm down," Nancy said softly. "I'm sure Mr. Harrison will understand."

"Oh, sure," Emily wailed. "He'll really believe me,

won't he! I might just as well tell him the dog ate my homework!"

"Well, you've still got your notes, right? You can rewrite it."

"It'll take weeks!" Emily sobbed. "I'd already written fourteen pages. And now they're gone."

Nancy handed her a tissue. Emily wiped her eyes. "So you accused Jessie of erasing your report?" Nancy asked. "Then what happened?"

"Then I totally lost it," Emily said, the words catching in her throat. "I don't know. I just went bananas. She made me so mad—"

"You know, you really have to go easy on Jessie," Nancy said, shoving the box of tissues into her sister's lap.

"Huh?"

"Jessie has a lot of problems," Nancy said. She pulled herself back onto the pillows and leaned against the headboard.

"What do you mean?" Emily was confused.

"Mom told me yesterday. She said Jessie has some serious emotional problems. She sees a shrink twice a week."

"Really? I didn't know that." Emily blew her nose. She was starting to feel a little steadier.

"I guess that was one of the hard adjustments for Jessie when she moved here," Nancy said, getting up and closing the bedroom door.

"You mean—"

"She had to leave her psychiatrist behind and find a new one here in Shadyside." Nancy resumed her place on the bed.

"How come? What kind of emotional problems?" Emily asked, whispering even though the door was now closed.

Nancy shrugged her narrow shoulders. "You know Mom. She wouldn't tell me. Mom never likes unpleasant details."

"Tell me about it!" Emily groaned, rolling her eyes. Her mother didn't even want to hear why she went berserk a few minutes ago. "She didn't tell you *anything?*"

"Well, she did a little." Nancy leaned forward and whispered, her face close to Emily's. Emily could smell peppermint on her breath. "She said Jessie got into serious trouble at her old school. Something really bad happened."

"What?" Emily asked eagerly.

"Mom didn't say."

"Didn't you ask her?"

"I wanted to," Nancy said, lying back on the bed. "But Rich came home just then. And that was the end of the conversation."

"Something really bad happened, huh? That's what Mom said? I'll bet that's why Jessie's mother was in such a hurry to send her here."

"Maybe," Nancy said. "We'll never get the details from Mom. Especially not now. Just be careful with her, Em. Try to keep out of her way—okay? She's a very troubled girl."

Emily started to say something, but the doorbell rang downstairs. "That must be Josh," she said, looking at the clock on Nancy's shelf. "Nine o'clock.

You know Josh—Mister Prompt." She pulled open the bedroom door. "Thanks for the talk, Nance."

Nancy shrugged. She looked just like their mother when she did that, Emily thought. Emily closed the door behind her and headed down to greet Josh. As she passed her room, she peeked inside and saw Jessie working intently on the computer. Emily continued down the stairs, thinking about Nancy's warning.

"Hi. Did you get your report finished?" Josh asked, wiping his work boots on the floor mat before following her into the living room. He tossed his down coat onto a chair and plopped down on the brown corduroy couch.

Emily sighed. "That's a long story."

She sat down beside him, thinking how glad she was to see him. He looks so cute, she thought. She loved his black, curly hair and his dark, intense eyes. He was short, at least an inch shorter than she, but it didn't bother her. He was so energetic, so fast-talking, so quick-moving that it somehow made up for his shortness of stature. He was wearing a gray and maroon Shadyside High sweatshirt and faded jeans. She just wanted to cuddle up with him and not say a word.

"Want to tell it to me?" he asked. "I'm in the mood for a long story."

"You just want to avoid studying," she said, giving him a playful shove.

A grin slowly spread across his face. He looks ten years old when he grins like that, she thought. "What have you got to eat?" he asked. He ate as much as ten boys, but somehow he stayed really skinny.

She took his hand and pulled him into the kitchen. She made him a bologna and Swiss cheese sandwich and loaded his plate up with potato chips. "Aren't you going to eat anything?" he asked.

"I don't eat six meals a day like you," she cracked.

"This is only my fifth," he replied, biting into the sandwich, getting mustard over his top lip. "Besides, this is just a snack. Are you going to tell me what happened to your report?"

"I guess." She pulled out a kitchen chair and scooted in across the table from him. She told him the whole story as she watched him eat the sandwich and potato chips. "Well, what do you think?" she asked when she was finished.

"I think I'd like to meet her," he joked. "She sounds really great."

"Very funny. Remind me later to laugh," she said sarcastically, and got up and headed to the living room.

He caught up with her and put his hands on her shoulders. "Sorry. Bad joke. I was just trying to keep it light."

"It isn't light. It's serious," Emily insisted. She pulled away from him and sat down on the couch.

"Well, I think you should wait until you're calm and then go discuss it with your mother."

"I can't," Emily said with some bitterness. "Mom never wants to hear about any problems. Especially now. She's off on cloud nine with her new husband. You should see them, making out like teenagers. It's really disgusting."

Josh leapt over the couch back into her lap. "Doesn't sound like a bad idea to me!"

Emily shoved him hard and he toppled to the floor. "The only person I have to confide in is Nancy," she said.

Josh looked up at her uncomfortably. He always looked uncomfortable whenever she mentioned Nancy. Maybe he feels guilty for dumping her, Emily thought. If he only knew that she had been about to dump *him*. Whenever Josh ran into Nancy at her house, they got along fine and chatted like old friends. But Emily could tell that Josh was nervous around Nancy and not really himself.

"Hey, are we going to study, or what?" Josh asked, picking up the trapper-keeper he had brought.

"I guess we can try," Emily said without enthusiasm.

Her mind was still on Jessie, on the fight they'd had, on having to face her again later. And she thought about Nancy's warning. What kind of bad trouble had Jessie been in? Emily wondered.

After less than an hour she slammed her textbook shut. "I can't concentrate," she said, tossing the book onto the floor.

Josh tossed his book down too. Then he slid closer to her and put his arm around her shoulders. He pulled her close to him. He felt so warm, so safe. His skin smelled sweet to Emily. She kissed him on the cheek, and then he turned her face and kissed her on the lips.

Suddenly she pulled away from him and uttered a

45

whispered cry. She had a funny feeling that they were being watched.

"What's wrong?" Josh whispered, moving to resume their kiss.

Emily looked toward the front stairway. The hall was dark, but in the shadows she could see someone watching them from the staircase.

Jessie.

She's taken over my room, she's wearing my clothes, and now she's spying on me, Emily thought angrily. Well, there's one thing of mine that she can't have—Josh. I hope the little Peeping Tom enjoys the show.

Emily reached up with both hands, pulled Josh's face to hers, closed her eyes, and kissed him with renewed passion.

A soft voice woke Emily from a deep sleep. She looked for the clock on her night-table, then remembered that the night-table was next to Jessie's bed now.

She closed her eyes, but the voice continued in a loud whisper. Jessie's voice. Emily was half-awake. It must be very late, she thought. The sky outside the bedroom window was black and starless.

In the darkness she could see Jessie on the other side of the room, sitting on the floor in the corner beside the desk. She was talking on the phone.

Who can she be calling this late at night? Emily wondered, her mind still fogged by sleep. She could just barely make out a few words Jessie was saying.

She seemed to be having an intense, whispered conversation with someone.

Who was it? What was she talking about so seriously, so heatedly?

Emily raised her head from the pillow to hear better.

"I could kill her," Jessie was saying into the phone. "I really could kill her."

chapter
5

Surprise in the Shower

Emily was standing right under the bell when it rang, signaling the end of the school day. She clapped her hands over her ears, dropping her books in the process, but it was too late. "I'm deaf for life!" she exclaimed.

"What did you say?" her friend Kathy joked, holding a hand up to her ear.

"Very funny." Emily bent down to pick up her books.

"How'd you do on the trig test?" Kathy asked, waving to someone across the hall.

"Good. Terrible. I don't know," Emily told her. The hall filled with kids. Lockers slammed. Voices echoed down the long tiled corridor. "Do you see Josh? He was supposed to meet me here."

"I don't see him. Hey—there's Della. Hey, Della—wait up!" Kathy shouted, and took off down the hall.

Standing up, Emily was bumped from behind and

nearly dropped her books again. "Sorry," a voice said. It was Ricky Schorr, loaded down with a tall stack of textbooks he was most likely taking to the book room.

"Hey, Ricky—can I borrow a quarter?" someone called. Everyone in earshot laughed.

Emily looked for Josh. He was always so punctual, she never could believe it when he was actually a minute or two late. She said hello to Lisa Blume and Cory Brooks, who were inseparable these days, then walked down the corridor and turned the corner where Josh's locker was. But he wasn't there either.

Finally she spotted him halfway down the hall. "Hey, Josh." But when she saw the girl he was talking to, Emily stopped short. Her words caught in her throat.

He was leaning against a locker, talking enthusiastically to Jessie, gesturing with his hands, smiling. The two of them were standing very close to each other. As Emily watched in surprise from down the hall, Josh said something, and he and Jessie burst out laughing.

"They're laughing at *me*," Emily told herself. "Hey —stop. Don't start getting paranoid."

But what was going on?

Emily had introduced Josh to Jessie a few days after their big fight. They had had a pleasant, short conversation, a little awkward but not too bad.

So what did they have to talk about now? And why had Josh completely forgotten about the fact that he was supposed to meet Emily?

"Hi, Emily."

Emily spun around, startled by the girl's voice. It was Krysta Meyers, a tiny, loud-voiced girl she never could stand. Krysta had become friends with Jessie. In fact, she was the only friend Jessie had made so far at Shadyside.

"Oh, hi, Krysta."

"Have you seen Jessie?" Krysta asked, squinting. She needed glasses but was too vain to wear them.

"She's right over there, talking to Josh," Emily said, pointing. She suddenly felt foolish, standing in the middle of the hall like a traffic director.

Krysta hurried off to collect Jessie. Emily watched the two girls walk off, then she hurried up to Josh. "Oh. Hi," he said, looking a little embarrassed. "Sorry, I didn't get over to you. I—"

"What were you and Jessie chatting about?" Emily asked. She didn't mean it to come out as accusing as it did.

"Nothing," Josh said, walking across the hall to his locker and starting to turn the combination lock.

"Nothing?"

"I was just talking to her," he said, pulling off the lock and opening the door. "I think she's lonely. She hasn't made any friends yet. Just Krysta."

"She *would* pick a girl I hate for a friend!" Emily exclaimed, and then immediately regretted it. "Wow. I sound really nasty today, don't I?"

Josh didn't reply. He had his head in his locker, searching for something. He probably hadn't even heard her.

"I thought you and Jessie were getting along better," he said, pulling his head out.

"Well, there hasn't been any bloodshed, if that's

what you mean," Emily said, frowning. "Actually, we've been pretty much giving each other a lot of space. It hasn't been too bad. She even helped me retype my report."

"Really? Maybe she's not a bad kid after all," Josh said, waving to some guys down the hall.

"Maybe . . ." Emily said doubtfully. Jessie was still making late-night phone calls every night. When Mr. Wallner had asked her if she had been on the phone late at night, Jessie had lied and said no.

"Hey, do we have to talk about Jessie all afternoon?" Emily asked, giving Josh a playful shove into his locker.

"No. Who should we talk about?" he asked, laughing.

"I thought we were going to talk about the Homecoming dance."

"Okay. What's to talk about?" He slammed his locker shut and locked it.

"Well, it *is* Friday night, you know."

"Right. I know, Em. I'll be there. How about you?" He laughed.

She didn't crack a smile. "Sometimes I think you take me for granted."

"That's okay," he said, leading the way out the door. "You can take me for granted too."

Can I? Emily wondered. She pictured him leaning so close to Jessie, talking and laughing with her in the hallway a few minutes before.

What *were* they talking about, anyway?

* * *

Two nights later, Jessie and Emily found themselves in the kitchen.

"Three canisters of whipped cream? Who bought *three* canisters?" Emily asked.

Jessie picked them up one by one and examined them as if searching for the answer to Emily's question. "Beats me. But I guess we have enough whipped cream to make this cake."

"Do we have the chocolate wafers?" Emily asked, standing on tiptoes to search the baking supplies cabinet over the stove.

"Probably not," Jessie replied. "Maybe we'll just make a whipped cream cake."

"I can't find the chocolate wafers. How can we make icebox cake without chocolate wafers?" Emily moaned.

Jessie flipped open one of the whipped cream canisters, pushed the top, and squirted a big, creamy blob of whipped cream into her mouth.

"Hey, stop—" Emily scolded. "We may need that."

Jessie laughed. "Three cans?! We couldn't eat three cans of whipped cream if we tried."

"I could!" Emily cracked. They both laughed.

Emily looked at the clock. Nine-thirty. "Come on, it's late," she said. "Why are we making a whipped cream cake this late? I've still got homework."

"Because we're *starving!*" Jessie declared. She shot another big blob of whipped cream into her mouth.

"But how can we do it without the chocolate wafers?" Emily complained. "Give me some of that." She opened her mouth wide.

Jessie turned the can around and pushed the top. The whipped cream squirted all over Emily's chin.

"Hey!"

"Sorry!" Jessie burst out laughing. Her blue eyes sparkled mischievously.

"This means war!" Emily declared, picking up a canister and pulling off the red plastic top.

"No, wait—wait—" Jessie raised her arms protectively and backed away from Emily. "That was an accident. Hey—this is a clean sweatshirt!"

Emily sent a spray of whipped cream up and down the front of Jessie's sweatshirt. "Z for Zorro! Olé!" she cried.

But Jessie was on the offensive before Emily's mouth closed. She shot a white blob of cream into Emily's mouth. "Bull's-eye!" she cried, and continued spraying until Emily's face was covered.

Both girls, laughing so hard they could barely stand, let go with long accurate barrages. "Hey—not so loud! Mom and Hugh are upstairs in their room!" Emily cried.

"Truce! Truce! It's all over the floor!" Jessie said, her sneakers sliding over a wet spot on the linoleum.

Emily moved forward on the attack, slipped, and fell on her face. Jessie immediately bent down and sprayed Emily's back. Now both girls were laughing too hard to shoot accurately. The whipped cream flew up to the kitchen window curtains.

"Uh-oh!"

This started them laughing hysterically. They were both down on the floor now.

This is the most fun I've had in ages, Emily thought, wiping whipped cream from her sneaker laces. Maybe Jessie isn't so bad after all. She's actually pretty terrific now that she's loosening up.

"*YAAIIII!*" Another full frontal attack from Jessie sent whipped cream all over the refrigerator door.

"What's going on in here?"

Both girls stopped and looked up to see Nancy stride into the kitchen in her striped pajamas, a bewildered look on her face.

"Let her have it!" Emily declared.

Nancy tried to back up, but she was hit full force by two streams of whipped cream at once. "Hey—my pajamas! My hair!" she cried, but Emily and Jessie didn't relent.

"Three can play at this," Nancy declared.

Emily reached for the third canister, but Nancy dived and got there first. She had trouble popping the lid off. The other two girls took full advantage of her trouble, spraying her nonstop.

The battle heated up when Nancy finally got her can to work. The only problem was, they were all laughing too hard now to aim accurately.

"You look ridiculous!" Jessie cried to Emily.

"You both look ridiculous! *I* look dignified!" Nancy declared.

"Get her!" Emily cried, letting loose a giant blast of whipped cream.

The great battle ended a few minutes later when all three cans were empty. "Now we can't have any cake," Emily complained.

"That's okay," Jessie said. She scooped a pile of

whipped cream off her sweatshirt and sucked it into her mouth. "I'm pretty full, actually."

"I've got to take a shower," Emily said, feeling the sticky stuff in her hair.

"We all do," Nancy said. She was sitting in the middle of the floor, surrounded by whipped cream.

"First we'd better clean up," Emily said.

"Tell you what," Jessie said to her, taking another mouthful of whipped cream. "You take the first shower. I'll start the cleanup. When you're done, come downstairs and help me finish."

"Really? Great!" Emily said. "Thanks, Jessie. You're a pal."

Emily pulled off her sneakers so she wouldn't track whipped cream all over the house and headed upstairs to take her shower. That was really nice of Jessie, she thought. She really is making an effort to make up for last week. It's like she's a changed person. I like this Jessie much better.

The hot water felt so good. Emily let it run through her hair for a long time. Amazing how quickly whipped cream starts to clot, she thought, rubbing in a big handful of shampoo.

I could stay in here forever, she thought. It's so warm and steamy.

But she remembered that Jessie was waiting for her to come downstairs and help, so she finished shampooing her hair, washed quickly, and stepped out of the shower. Humming to herself, feeling very refreshed, she walked over to the mirror. It was steamed up, rivulets of water trickling down.

Emily picked up a towel and rubbed it across the

mirror to wipe away the steam. She peered into the mirror.

Then she screamed.

And screamed again.

She had the feeling she might never stop screaming.

chapter
6

Emily's New Look

*E*mily was still screaming when the bathroom door swung open. Nancy, looking very frightened, burst into the steamy bathroom, followed by a gust of cold air.

"Em—what's the matter?"

"My hair! My hair!" Emily shrieked, pulling wildly at her wet, tangled hair with both hands, staring into the mirror.

"Here—put this on." Nancy slipped a bathrobe over Emily's shoulders. "Go ahead. Pull it tight."

"My hair! Look at my hair!"

"Emily, stop screaming like that. Please—take your hands away so that I can see what you're talking about."

Emily lowered her hands to tie the robe. She shivered from the cold air entering the bathroom through the open door.

Their mother hurried in, followed by Jessie and Mr.

Wallner. They all had to squeeze into the small, narrow bathroom.

"Em—your hair! What did you do?" Mrs. Wallner cried.

They could all see the ugly orange and yellow splotches and streaks.

"What did *I* do?!" Emily exploded. "I didn't do *anything!* And look!"

"How strange!" Mr. Wallner said, coming close to examine her hair.

"It's ruined forever!" Emily wailed, turning away from the mirror.

"You've bleached it somehow," Mrs. Wallner said, holding a strand in her fingers, pulling it up close to her face.

"Me? Why do you keep saying *I* did it?" Emily shrieked. "All I did was shampoo my hair. And now look—"

The left side was almost entirely orange. The front was streaked with uneven lines of greenish yellow. The rest of her hair was dotted with blotches of orange and yellow.

"It—it's ruined. My hair is ruined!" Emily cried, keeping her head lowered so she wouldn't have to see herself in the mirror.

Mrs. Wallner put her arms around her daughter and tried to comfort her.

"How weird," Jessie said from near the door.

Mr. Wallner had picked up the plastic shampoo bottle and was sniffing it. "Did you just buy this shampoo?"

"No," Emily sobbed. "I've had it for weeks. The

bottle was only a third full." She buried her head in her mother's side.

"We have to take it to the store," Mrs. Wallner said. "Maybe somebody tampered with it—"

"But she's been using it for weeks," Mr. Wallner interrupted, pouring some of the green shampoo into his hand.

"But there's something wrong with it," Mrs. Wallner insisted. "Look at her. I've never seen anything like it."

"Mom—" Nancy started, a warning to her mother to be careful of what she said. Emily was just starting to calm down a little.

"Hey, wait." Mr. Wallner bent down and picked something up out of the wastebasket under the sink. "Look at this." He held up a small brown bottle.

"What's that?" Jessie asked.

"It's a bottle of peroxide," Mr. Wallner said, his expression turning even more grim. "It's empty." He turned it upside down.

"You mean—" Nancy started.

"Peroxide?" Emily was so upset, she couldn't follow what was going on. Everyone was a blur, a steamy blur. She shivered under the bathrobe and tried to bring them all into focus. But her eyes just wouldn't clear.

Mr. Wallner tilted the shampoo bottle and let the shampoo run into the sink. "Somebody emptied the peroxide into Emily's shampoo."

"But who would do that?" Jessie asked, sounding horrified.

"We have to find out. This is serious," he said,

studying the green shampoo as it ran down the white porcelain sink.

"Jessie spent an awfully long time in the bathroom just before dinner," Nancy said.

All eyes turned on Jessie, whose face immediately turned angry. "So what does that prove?" She glared at Nancy.

"I didn't accuse you," Nancy said, crossing her arms in front of her chest. "I just said—"

"Why would I do such a horrible thing?" Jessie shrieked.

"Calm down, Jessie!" Mr. Wallner shouted. "Nancy shouldn't have said that."

"But it's true," Nancy insisted. "I tried to get into the bathroom for twenty minutes, but Jessie—"

"I didn't do it!" Jessie cried, moving menacingly toward Nancy.

Her father quickly stepped between them.

"Jessie, calm down. No one said—"

"You all think I did it, don't you?" Jessie asked, looking from one face to the next. "Everyone thinks that because of what happened to Jolie that I—that I'm a horrible person who would do anything. That *is* what you think—isn't it?"

Jolie?

Who's Jolie? Emily wondered, searching Jessie's angry face as if trying to find the answer there.

Who is Jolie, and what happened to her?

"Jessie, stop screaming. Everybody . . . stop screaming," Mr. Wallner said, slamming his hands against the sides of the sink.

"I get accused of everything that happens around

here!" Jessie cried, ignoring him. "And I know why too. Don't think I don't know why." These last words were spoken to her father.

She did it, Emily realized.

Jessie did it. She put the peroxide in my shampoo. Now she's carrying on and throwing a tantrum so that no one will be able to accuse her, to make her confess.

But she's gone too far, Emily thought. She's not that good an actress. She got too angry too fast. That's the giveaway. She's the one who did this to me.

As Emily thought this, Nancy and Jessie screamed accusations back and forth. Mr. Wallner shouted at them to stop. Mrs. Wallner smoothed Emily's discolored hair back off her forehead.

"Everyone hates me!" Jessie cried, her hands clenched in tight fists, her blue eyes wide and flashing in fury.

"What's wrong with this family?" Mrs. Wallner wailed. "Why can't we get along? Why can't we discuss this like—"

"Everybody just be silent for thirty seconds!" Mr. Wallner bellowed, making a pleading gesture with his big hands, his face bright red.

"Jessie, why are you being so defensive?" Nancy asked quietly, ignoring her stepfather's request.

"Everyone hates me! No one believes me!" Jessie shrieked. She turned and ran out of the bathroom, crying at the top of her lungs.

Even her crying sounds phony, Emily decided. Such hysterics. But Jessie can't quite pull it off. She isn't fooling anyone. At least, she isn't fooling me.

"Where's Rich?" Nancy asked suddenly.

Mr. Wallner looked at Mrs. Wallner. "If that boy is responsible for this . . ."

"Don't *you* start getting crazy," Mrs. Wallner told her husband, taking his arm. "We have no reason to suspect Rich. He went to the library right after dinner."

"He should be home by now, shouldn't he?" Nancy asked, looking at her watch.

"Yes, he should," her mother replied. "It's strange. It's not like Rich to stay out so late."

"What about my hair?" Emily wailed, catching a glimpse of the spotted mess in the mirror.

Nancy put her arm around her sister's shoulders and started to guide her out the door. "Come to my room," she said softly. "Let's see what we can do with it. Maybe we can make it look deliberate. You know. Sort of punky, sort of cutting edge."

Emily gratefully let her sister guide her out into the hall. Behind her she could hear her parents arguing about whether Rich was the culprit or not. As she passed her bedroom, she saw Jessie sitting on her bed, writing furiously in her diary, sobbing loudly.

Not very convincing, Jessie, Emily thought.

Not very convincing at all.

Jessie ruined my hair.

It had to be Jessie.

A horrifying thought made Emily's breath catch in her throat.

What would Jessie do next?

chapter

7

Murder

"*I like your hair," Nancy said, getting up from her desk. She was wearing faded jeans and a man's striped shirt.

"Thanks," Emily said. "You did a great job, Nance. Trimming the sides so short was a real inspiration."

"You're right. It was, if I do say so myself."

"It really looks like I put in blond highlights. I wonder if Josh will like it," Emily said, feeling a sudden flutter of nervousness.

"He hasn't seen it?"

"No. He wasn't in school yesterday or today. Some kind of virus or something. He says he's fine now."

"Knowing Josh," Nancy said, "he won't even notice."

Emily laughed. "What a mean thing to say." She thought about it. "But you're right, of course."

"I'm always right," Nancy said, smiling. "Hey, you're not dressed."

"I'll get dressed after dinner. Hugh is making spaghetti with his famous tomato sauce. I don't want to go to the basketball game and the dance with big orange blobs all over my clothes."

Nancy turned away suddenly and looked out the window, as if avoiding Emily's gaze. "I had a date," she said wistfully. "But he had to go out of town with his parents at the last minute."

Poor Nancy, Emily thought. She keeps getting stood up by guys. She just can't seem to find anyone who's really interested in her.

"It's just as well," Nancy said, turning her gaze back on Emily. "I have so much studying to do. I'll be able to get a good head start on it tonight while you're out wasting your time having fun." She laughed.

"Bitter, bitter," Emily said gently, not as a criticism.

Nancy started to say something, but they were interrupted by a commotion downstairs. They both heard a loud pounding on the front door, followed by hurried footsteps across the hall, followed by loud, troubled voices.

"Now what?" Nancy asked, rolling her eyes.

They both headed for the stairs.

Halfway down the staircase Emily was startled to see a tall policeman in the front hall. He had his hand firmly on Rich's shoulder. Rich, in his blue down vest with a gray sweatshirt underneath and blue corduroys, was squirming under the policeman's grip, looking very pale and frightened. He looked up at Emily and Nancy as they descended the stairs, and Emily saw that he had a dark spot of dried blood above his lip.

"Did you *hit* him?" Emily sputtered, startled by the sight of the blood.

"What?" The policeman, a young man with the beginnings of a brown mustache on his lip, looked up, confused by her question.

"No," Rich muttered to the floor. "I had a nosebleed in school this afternoon."

Mr. Wallner, in a stained white apron, a large wooden mixing spoon in his hand, stood staring angrily at Rich. "The officer has informed me that Rich committed a crime this evening."

"What!" Jessie came bounding down the stairs. She stopped behind Emily and Nancy, who leaned against the banister on the bottom. "Rich, what did you do?"

"Nothing much," Rich muttered, looking down at his sneakers, both of which were untied, as usual.

"Don't say that," the officer warned. He had a thin, reedy voice that made him sound about twelve years old. "Shoplifting is a serious offense, son."

"Shoplifting?" Jessie cried, looking very alarmed.

"Rich was caught stealing a cassette from the record store in the Division Street Mall," Mr. Wallner informed them. "He had it in his vest pocket."

"I meant to pay for it," Rich said with a sneer.

"Don't make it even worse by lying," Mr. Wallner snapped.

"Maybe he isn't lying," Jessie said.

Emily looked at her, surprised. It was the first time she had ever heard Jessie stand up for her brother.

"The manager isn't pressing charges," the policeman said to Mr. Wallner. "Since the boy is so young, he just figured you should probably be the one to deal with the problem." He let go of Rich's shoulder.

"Oh, don't worry about it," said Mr. Wallner, glaring at Rich. "I'll deal with it, okay. When I'm *finished* dealing with it, I don't think Rich will ever *think* of shoplifting again."

Rich made a disgusted face that Emily could see but his father couldn't.

"Why'd you do it, Rich?" Mr. Wallner asked, softening a little.

Rich shrugged.

"I've got to be going," the policeman said, running a finger over his burgeoning mustache. "Stay out of trouble, son. Okay?"

Rich nodded.

The policeman turned and left quickly, the glass storm door slamming behind him. A burst of cold air entered the hallway, but the atmosphere inside was even colder than the winter air.

"Why'd you do it?" Mr. Wallner demanded. "Why?"

"I'm sorry," Rich said, his voice cracking.

"If you wanted a cassette, why didn't you ask me for the money?" his father demanded.

"Sorry," Rich said. He raised his eyes and stared at Mr. Wallner, as if to show that he wasn't afraid of him.

"But why steal? What would make you think you had to steal?"

"Sorry," Rich repeated. Each time he repeated the word, it made Mr. Wallner even angrier.

Rich probably knows that, Emily thought. What a strange boy he is.

"But, Rich—"

"Sorry, sorry, sorry."

"Leave him alone," Jessie interrupted, pushing her way past Emily and Nancy. "Can't you see he's too upset to talk about it?" She put her arm around Rich's shoulders.

Rich started to move away, then changed his mind. He stood in place, looking uncomfortable.

Jessie really cares about her brother, Emily thought.

Or is this some kind of show she's putting on?

No. She seems sincere this time. Not like the other night.

Emily and Jessie had barely exchanged two words since the shower incident two nights before.

"Oh, no—my sauce!" Mr. Wallner cried, suddenly reminded by the spoon in his hands. He hurried back to the kitchen. "Rich, we'll have a long talk after dinner," he called as he ran.

"Can't wait," Rich muttered, loud enough for everyone but his father to hear.

"Bad attitude," Jessie said quietly, removing her arm from around his shoulder. "That bad attitude will really get you into trouble, Rich."

"What do *you* know about it?" Rich snapped angrily. Before Jessie could react, he pushed past the three girls and fled up the stairs, two at a time.

Mrs. Wallner returned home a few minutes later. Emily could hear her stepdad telling her the whole story in the kitchen.

Needless to say, dinner was solemn and nearly silent. Rich asked to be excused after only a few forkfuls of spaghetti.

"My kids," Mr. Wallner complained to no one in particular, shaking his head. "What am I raising?"

Emily looked over at Jessie, who was glaring back at her father, a hurt expression on her face, cold fury in her eyes.

Shadyside won the basketball game with a foul shot in the final seconds. The score was 49 to 48. The shouts and cheers and raucous blasts from the school band at the final whistle were so loud, Emily thought the old gym might burst at the seams.

Jessie had gone to the game even though she didn't have a date for the dance afterward. Emily saw her once, walking with Krysta up to the top row of the bleachers, the two of them chattering away.

She's so silent at home, Emily thought. I wonder how many different personalities she has. I'll never really get to know Jessie, she thought wistfully. Then she remembered her anger—and her fear. I don't really *want* to know Jessie, she told herself, and shut all thoughts of her stepsister from her mind.

Nancy had been right about Josh. If Emily hadn't pointed out her new hairstyle, he never would have noticed. "I like it a lot," he had said. But then he had added, "Really," which meant that Emily couldn't believe him.

The dance in the auditorium, decorated with dozens of paper tulips, was fairly crowded for a school dance. It was the big dance of the year, after all. But school dances in general weren't very well attended. There wasn't much school spirit at Shadyside. Kids didn't seem to have much time for old-fashioned things like a Homecoming dance. Most of them would rather be cruising around town in their cars or partying in someone's living room with their parents away.

"Do you think I'm really out-of-it for wanting to come to this dance?" Emily asked Josh, shouting in his ear as they stood on the side of the dance floor, watching kids dance to a loud, insistent rap song.

"I think you're very retro," he said, grinning.

"That means backward, doesn't it?" she joked.

"It means out-of-it," he said.

She excused herself to go to the girls' room. On her way across the dimly lit auditorium, she bumped into Jessie's friend Krysta. Actually, it seemed to Emily that Krysta had deliberately approached her.

"Hi!" Krysta called enthusiastically.

"Oh, hi, Krysta." Emily didn't feel like returning the enthusiasm. "Where's Ben?" Ben Ashworth was about the richest kid at Shadyside High. His family had a huge mansion overlooking the river in North Hills. His father owned shopping malls or something. Krysta had latched on to Ben the first day he arrived at school, and in Emily's view, she hadn't let him out of her sight since.

"He's getting us something to drink," Krysta said, glancing over to the refreshment table. "Emily, I love your hair."

"Oh. Thanks," Emily said, unable to keep the suspicion from her voice.

"It's totally different, isn't it," Krysta said, admiring it. "I love the color. And you cut it short too. It's really great."

"Thanks," Emily said uncomfortably. "I've got to go. See you later."

"Too bad Jessie didn't get a date," Krysta called after her as Emily continued on quickly toward the girls' room.

Emily didn't bother to reply. She was seething with anger. It was obvious that Jessie had told Krysta about putting the peroxide in the shampoo. The two of them must have had a big laugh at Emily's expense. Krysta must have known all about Jessie's vicious prank. Why else would she have deliberately come up to Emily to rave and carry on so long about Emily's hair?

The more Emily thought about it, the angrier she got. If Jessie told Krysta what she had done, then Krysta must have told the whole school. Everyone in the auditorium tonight probably knew why Emily had this weird new short haircut.

But surely no one else would think it was funny, would they?

Everyone would agree with Emily that it was vicious, terrifyingly vicious—wouldn't they?

Emily tried to enjoy the rest of the dance, but she couldn't stop thinking about all this. She tried dancing her thoughts away, losing herself in the throbbing rhythms, the music so deafeningly loud that the old auditorium floor actually vibrated from it.

"Pump it! Come on—pump it! Pump it up! Pump it up!" the song insisted.

It helped for a while.

The repetition of the words, the pounding, pounding, pounding of the synthesized drums, carried her away, away from her thoughts, away from Josh even, until she was floating on the vibrating, pulsing sounds.

It ended all too soon.

The wet chill of the night air as they walked to Josh's car brought her back to reality. Their feet crunched loudly over the hard ground. She grabbed on to his arm and held on tightly, leaning against him as they walked.

Parked in her driveway, she lingered, kissing him passionately. She didn't want to go home, didn't want to go inside. She wanted to stay with Josh.

But that was impossible, of course.

It was after one-thirty when she dragged herself out of the steamy car and up the walk to her front door. She pulled her coat around her as the cold air made her shiver. Josh's headlights came on, throwing a harsh yellow light on the front of the house. She waved to him and closed the front door behind her.

The house was dark and silent. Everyone had gone to bed. A dim hall light upstairs provided the only light.

Emily pulled off her coat and tossed it over the back of a living-room chair. Yawning silently, she pulled off her shoes. She could still taste Josh on her lips. She smiled to herself in the darkness, then stopped short.

That's odd, she thought. Where's Tiger?

The little dog was a very light sleeper. No matter how late it was, he always came running out to greet her from his sleeping spot by the heat register in the kitchen.

So where was he?

"Tiger?" she whispered. Where could he be?

Had Nancy taken him upstairs to sleep with her? It was possible. But she hadn't done that in years.

"Tiger?"

Her throat suddenly felt very dry. Emily headed to the kitchen to get a glass of water. "Tiger, are you in here?"

Where could that silly dog be?

Walking in her stocking feet over the linoleum, she turned on the light over the sink. She was about to open the cabinet door to get a glass when she saw him.

"Oh, no! Oh, *no!*"

chapter
8

In Hot Water

Emily sank to her knees beside the dog.

Tiger was lying on his back. He was dead. His eyes had already sunk into his head.

"Oh, no! Oh, no!"

He had a large wound in his chest, straight like a cut. It was a cut. A deep cut.

Tiger must have been stabbed. He lay in a dark pool of drying blood.

"Oh, no. No, no, no."

Emily picked the little dog up in her arms, blood trickling down the front of her white sweater.

There's a killer in this house, Emily thought. We're living with a killer.

She pictured Tiger bounding across the floor, his little legs moving like a speeded-up movie, his stubby tail switching from side to side. Then she pictured Jessie angrily kicking at him, Jessie angrily tossing him hard to the floor.

Jessie hated Tiger.

There's a killer in this house.

"Help me!" Emily screamed. "Somebody—help me!"

Mrs. Wallner came running down the stairs first, followed by her husband.

"Help me! Please!"

They were followed by Nancy, Jessie, and Rich, all in pajamas, all wide-eyed, frightened-looking, all forcing themselves awake.

When they burst into the kitchen, Emily was still holding the corpse in her arms, her hands covered with blood.

"Tiger!" Nancy screamed.

"What on earth—!"

"Emily—are you okay?"

"Tiger's dead," Emily said, unnecessarily.

"Ugh. Put it down," Jessie pleaded.

Mrs. Wallner leaned against the kitchen counter, trying to catch her breath. She looked as white as the Formica countertop, and under the harsh fluorescent glare of the overhead light, she looked older than usual, and tired, streaks of gray showing in her coppery hair.

"Someone must have broken in," she said, keeping her head down, avoiding having to look at Tiger.

"But who would break in just to murder a dog?" Emily cried.

"Put it down! Put it down!" Jessie shrieked.

"No sign of any break-in," Mr. Wallner said after checking all the windows. "Here, Em, let me take that."

He reached for the dog's body, but Emily turned away, refusing to give it up.

"Your sweater—it's ruined," Nancy said, tears in her eyes.

Emily looked at Rich. His blond hair was matted against his forehead. His pajama shirt had ridden up, revealing a few inches of pale stomach. His eyes looked red and bloodshot.

He looked away, avoiding her gaze. He hadn't uttered a cry. In fact, he hadn't said a word.

"Emily, let me have the dog," Mr. Wallner said gently.

Emily relented. He took the dog from her arms and carried it away. "Where are you taking him?" Emily called after him.

"Just to the back stoop. I'll call the ASPCA in the morning. They'll come and take him away." He pulled open the kitchen door with his free hand and stepped outside in his pajamas.

"It's so awful," Jessie said, dropping down onto one of the tall stools in front of the counter. "Who would do such a horrible thing?"

Emily glared accusingly at her. "You never liked Tiger."

Jessie's mouth dropped open. "You're not accusing *me*, are you?"

"You never liked Tiger," Emily repeated. She tried to clear her mind, but the picture of the murdered dog wouldn't fade from view. She kept seeing it over and over. She felt as if she were in a dream, where everything repeated and repeated. "You never liked

75

Tiger." Had she already said that? Hadn't this all happened before? Several times before?

Was it happening now?

"No, I don't like dogs," Jessie said. "But I wouldn't kill an innocent animal!"

"Somebody did," Nancy said in a flat, weary voice.

"I don't see what good it will do to stand here and accuse each other," Mrs. Wallner said. She moved forward and put her arms around Emily.

"But someone in this room murdered Tiger!" Emily cried. "We have to know who did it. We have to."

"Maybe it was an accident," her mother said. "Maybe Tiger fell on something. Something sharp."

"Fell on what?" Mr. Wallner asked.

"I—I just don't want to believe that someone in this house could have—could have—" Mrs. Wallner's words choked in her throat.

Of course not, Emily thought. Mom never wants to believe anything bad about anybody. She doesn't want to believe that Jessie is capable of killing. But the evidence is so clear.

She looked over to Nancy. Her sister had her arms crossed tightly over her chest, as if trying to hold her feelings in, as if trying to hold herself together. "I heard Rich walking around earlier tonight," Nancy said.

"I got up to get a drink of water," Rich whined, his voice cracking. His first words of the night.

"Rich, if you did this," Mr. Wallner said quietly, looking down at the dark puddle of blood on the linoleum, "tell us now. If you need help from us, let us

76

know. You won't be punished. I promise. We'll get you the help you need." He said this softly, caringly.

Emily was surprised. It wasn't the way her stepfather usually reacted. He usually barreled into a situation without thinking of anyone's feelings, especially Rich's. But this was serious, and Mr. Wallner was treating it that way.

"But I didn't *do* it!" Rich cried, his voice rising several octaves. He suddenly looked very frightened.

"This isn't right. We can't just stand here and accuse each other," Mrs. Wallner said.

"That book you've been reading," Nancy said to Rich. *"Pet Sematary?* I read that. It's about a pet that dies. And then the people bring it back from the dead."

"So *what?"* Rich shouted. "So *what?"*

"Rich, I mean what I said," Mr. Wallner said, staring at his trembling son. "You won't be punished. I promise. Just tell us the truth."

"I *am* telling the truth!" Rich cried. "I'm not a killer! Just because I read books doesn't mean I'm a killer!" He turned and fled from the room. They could hear him running up the stairs. Then they heard his bedroom door slam.

"I think we should all go to bed and try to get a little sleep," Mrs. Wallner said, holding on to her husband's arm, gripping it so tightly, Mr. Wallner winced.

"How can we sleep?" Emily cried.

"Maybe Rich needs to see a shrink too," Mr. Wallner said suddenly, lost in his own thoughts. "But I don't see how I can afford to send two kids to the shrink."

Emily saw Jessie blush. No one in the family was supposed to know that Jessie was seeing a shrink.

"Everything will be clearer in the morning," Mrs. Wallner said, tugging at her husband's arm.

"But we have a real serious problem on our hands," Mr. Wallner insisted.

"But, Hugh—"

"Okay," he said, scratching his bald head. "Go on upstairs, dear. I'll just clean up the floor, and then I'll be up."

"I'm going up too," Jessie said and disappeared from the room.

"You want me to stay downstairs and we'll talk?" Nancy asked Emily.

"No. I guess not," Emily said. She didn't know what she wanted. She wanted for this not to have happened. "Go on back to sleep, Nance."

"I don't think any of us will sleep tonight," Nancy said sadly. But she turned and, still hugging herself, headed up to her room.

Mr. Wallner headed to the broom closet to get a mop.

"Jessie did it," Emily told her mother, who had hesitated at the door.

"What?"

"You heard me, Mom. Jessie did it. I know she did. She hated Tiger. She hates me."

"Emily—" her mother started, then stopped. She was thinking hard, trying to figure out what to say. "Why do you accuse Jessie of everything?"

"Because she's the one who's doing these terrible things," Emily said softly, slowly, suddenly feeling

78

very sleepy despite the horror, despite the picture of the dead dog that wouldn't leave her mind.

"But you have no proof. Just because you have a hunch—"

"It's *not* a hunch. I *know* it's Jessie!" Emily shouted, feeling the anger rise, catching her throat, making her feel about to cry. "You don't really know her, Mom. She's different from what you think she is. She acts real sweet when you're around. But then when we're alone, she—"

"You've got to ask yourself why you are always trying to blame Jessie," her mother said. "Are you jealous of her for some reason? You shouldn't be. You know, Jessie is your sister now and—"

"Mother, *why won't you ever listen to me?*" Emily screamed.

"But I *am* listening, dear. I know that you and Jessie are having problems. Maybe the three of us should sit down and have a long talk. We could—"

"Oh, what's the point?" Emily cried, out of control and unable to do anything about it. Tears ran down her cheeks. She ran past her mother to the stairs.

Her mother made no attempt to stop her or call her back.

She has no intention of ever confronting Jessie, Emily thought bitterly as she climbed the stairs. She always thinks if she ignores things, they'll simply go away. When Daddy died, she was no help at all. Nancy and I had to do everything. She's the child in the family. We're all grown-ups compared to Mom.

The light was on in her room. Emily stopped at the doorway.

What was she going to say to Jessie?

How could she go to sleep in the same room with the girl who had murdered her dog?

I'll call the police, she thought.

No. The police wouldn't be interested in a murdered dog. Or would they? They might. Except . . . Except her mother was right. Emily didn't have any proof.

And what if it was Rich? That weirdo with his Stephen King books. He had already been caught committing one crime. Was he capable of killing a dog?

"Emily?"

"Oh!" Jessie had come up from behind in the hallway, startling Emily.

"Sorry. I didn't mean to frighten you. I was in the bathroom. You must be so upset. I'm running you a hot bath."

"You are?" Emily felt totally confused. She was prepared for an angry confrontation with her stepsister. And here was Jessie acting so concerned.

"A hot bath will make you feel better," Jessie said softly. "And you can wash off all the blood."

"Thanks, Jess. I—"

"Go get undressed. It's almost ready. I used a lot of that bath oil you like." She gave Emily a gentle push into the bedroom, then headed across the hall to tend to the bathwater.

Emily stood in the middle of the bedroom, feeling somewhat dazed. Why was Jessie being so nice to her? To cover up her guilt?

She kicked off her shoes, then pulled off the bloodstained sweater. She crumpled it in a ball and tossed it into a corner.

She heard her mother come up the stairs and stop at her bedroom door. "Em—you going to be okay?"

"Yes, Mother," she told her without turning around. "Get some sleep."

Her mother padded down the hallway to her room.

Something caught Emily's eye on the counter Jessie used for a desk. She walked over to it. It was Jessie's diary.

Emily listened to the water still running into the tub. She picked up the diary. It was a fat, leather-bound book with a metal clasp. The clasp was open. Jessie had left the diary unlocked.

Curious, Emily flipped back through the pages, glancing at the doorway to make sure Jessie wasn't returning. The diary seemed to cover several years. In her tiny, precise handwriting, Jessie had faithfully filled in just about every day.

Reading quickly, not finding anything terribly interesting, Emily heard footsteps in the hall. She slammed the book back down on the counter and took a step back.

But it was only her stepfather on his way to bed.

Breathing hard, she picked up the diary again. Her eyes settled on a long, upsetting passage from just a few days before. "Emily blamed me again," Jessie had written. "I don't know what to do about her. But I've got to do something."

The tub water stopped. Emily closed the diary. She realized she was trembling.

I've got to read more, she thought.

I've got to know what Jessie is planning. I've got to know just how dangerous she is.

She carried the diary quickly over to her bed and hid it under her pillow. I'll wait till Jessie is asleep, and then I'll read more, she thought.

"Aren't you undressed yet? The water is ready." Jessie stepped into the room, drying her wet hands on the front of her pajamas.

"Oh. Thanks." Emily didn't move.

"Emily—are you okay?" Jessie asked, putting a warm hand on her shoulder. The touch of Jessie's hand drove the swirling thoughts from Emily's mind. "Go take your bath. You'll feel better."

"Okay. You're being very nice, Jessie."

"I just feel so bad," Jessie said.

Emily finished getting undressed in the bathroom, then stopped at the edge of the tub. The bathwater smelled so good. Jessie had used a lot of the lilac bath oil Emily loved. The room was so steamy, warm, and comforting.

Emily looked down at the brown bloodstains on her hands and arms. "Got to wash this away."

But as she prepared to step into the tub, she was stopped by a stab of fear. Cold fear.

The water.

What had Jessie done to the water?

She had poured peroxide into the shampoo. She had deliberately ruined Emily's hair with that dreadful trick.

Emily stared down into the steaming bathwater, suddenly feeling sick, feeling heavy, so heavy, weighed down by fear, paralyzed by her realization that something was wrong here.

Was the water scalding hot?

Was that Jessie's trick for tonight?

Or had she poured something horrible into the water? Some kind of acid that would eat away all of Emily's flesh and leave her skeleton soaking in the tub?

The water was blue-green from the bath oil.

But what else was in there? What was the blue-green color supposed to hide?

Emily stared down into the water, wondering what Jessie had in store for her.

chapter
9

The Late-Night Visitor

*T*he bathwater looked so blue. So still. So deadly.

I can't do it, Emily thought.

She washed the blood off her hands and arms in the sink, dried quickly with a hand towel, then pulled on the nightshirt she had carried into the bathroom with her and walked back to her bedroom. Jessie looked up from her bed, a *People* magazine in her hands. "What's wrong?"

"I—uh—can't."

"Huh?"

"I'm too tired and too upset," Emily said. "It was really nice of you, but I think I just want to go to bed."

"Oh." Jessie looked disappointed. She tossed the magazine onto the floor and stood up. "Might as well not let it go to waste," she said, and hurried past Emily to the bathroom.

A few seconds later Emily heard the splash of Jessie

sitting down in the bathtub. The water was perfectly okay.

Okay, okay. So I misjudged her this time, Emily thought, wearily pulling down the covers of her bed.

Jessie was obviously being nice now to throw her off-guard.

Again, Emily saw the blood, saw her poor Tiger lying with that long, straight cut across his chest.

She shivered. It was so cold sleeping by the window. Why had she allowed Jessie to bully her and take away her bed by the wall? She hadn't slept comfortably ever since Jessie had arrived.

How could she sleep comfortably? Jessie was a murderer.

I've got to stop thinking, Emily told herself, feeling the diary under her pillow. I've got to shut off my mind, or I'll never get to sleep, never be able to think clearly again.

She shut her eyes tightly and tried to drive away all of the horrid pictures that kept flashing across her mind. From across the hall she heard the sound of the tub plug being pulled and the gurgle of the water starting to drain from the tub.

Then she was floating, floating dizzily in the dark, the room spinning, spinning so fast, spinning her to sleep.

She was awakened a short while later by a hand gripping her shoulder. She raised her head and uttered a short cry, startled. "What?"

It was dark, so dark she couldn't see a thing. That's odd, she thought, suddenly frightened. Usually some light comes in through the window.

The hand gripped her shoulder tightly and shook her.

"Let go," Emily said, her voice choked with sleep. "Who is it?"

The hand let go. A lamp clicked on. It was Jessie. She was sitting on the edge of Emily's bed. Her crinkly blond hair was wild and disheveled. Her eyes, usually so pale blue, were dark and alive.

"Wake up, Emily. You've slept long enough," Jessie whispered. Her wide grin was frightening.

"What? What's the matter?" Emily struggled to wake up, to clear her mind, but it was like swimming underwater. She struggled and struggled, but couldn't get to the surface.

The bedroom light seemed to flicker and dim.

"How long have I been asleep?" Emily asked.

"Not long." Jessie leaned down over her, still grinning.

Emily saw a shadow behind Jessie. Someone else was in the room.

"Who's that?" Emily asked.

The light seemed to brighten. Krysta stepped into view. "Hi, Emily. Sorry about this," she said. She was grinning too, grinning at Jessie.

It was some sort of a conspiracy, Emily realized. But what? What was Krysta doing in her room in the middle of the night?

"I love your hair," Krysta said. And both girls laughed loudly. Krysta stepped closer. She was still wearing the dress she had on at the dance.

Then Emily saw the knife in Jessie's hand.

It was a big black-handled kitchen knife. The blade was smeared with dark red blood.

"Hey!" Emily still felt as if she were swimming underwater. "Hey—what are you doing?"

"You know," Jessie said.

"I love your hair," Krysta said. "Really."

"Jessie—wait!" Emily cried.

Jessie raised the knife. The blade was so red, so dripping red.

"Jessie—no!"

Jessie held the knife over Emily's head with one hand and gripped her shoulder with the other hand.

"No—please!"

Gripping her shoulder harder, she began to shake Emily.

Emily closed her eyes and waited for the knife blade to drop.

I'm dead, she thought. Jessie has killed me. I'm dead. Dead, dead, dead.

Then she woke up.

It was a dream.

A frightening dream.

The room was pitch-black.

And someone was gripping her shoulder.

chapter

10

Packing It In

"**No!**" Emily tried to scream, but no sound came out.

"Shhhh. It's me," said a familiar voice. He let go of her shoulder.

Emily squinted in the darkness, her heart pounding. "Rich?"

"Yeah."

She turned and sat up. The nightmare still hovered over her like a heavy cloud. It had seemed so real. She could still see the bloodstained knife blade, so red, so deadly red.

"Rich—what's the matter? What do you want?"

His face moved out of the shadows, pale gray in the dim light from the window. He looked very nervous.

"Sorry. I didn't mean to scare you."

"But what do you want?" she insisted. This was so weird. Rich never came into their room. What was he doing here now, shaking her like that, waking her up in the middle of the night?

"I didn't kill your dog," Rich said in a loud whisper.

"What?"

"That's what I wanted to tell you. I didn't kill your dog." He moved even closer. His eyes peered into hers as if trying to determine whether or not she believed him.

"Rich, please. It's so late." The room was spinning. His face, so close to hers, was spinning with it.

"I didn't kill Tiger. I liked him. Really. Please believe me."

He had tears in his eyes. It seemed so terribly important to him that Emily believe him. "I believe you," Emily said wearily.

She wasn't really sure whether she believed him or not.

The nightmare flashed through her mind once again. And once again she saw Jessie holding the bloody kitchen knife. "Go back to sleep, Rich. I believe you."

"Thanks," he said, turning his head so she wouldn't see the tears.

That's an odd thing to say, she thought. Thanks? He's so grateful to me for believing him?

"Thanks," he repeated, and disappeared into the darkness.

Emily sat up, hoping it would make the room stop spinning. It helped a little. Why was it so cold in the room?

She looked over to Jessie's bed. Jessie was such a light sleeper. Any little sound would wake her. Why hadn't she awakened when Rich had come into the room?

Hey—wait. "Jessie?"

Emily thought maybe her eyes were playing tricks on her. She climbed out of bed, feeling even colder away from the covers. She took a few steps across the room toward Jessie's bed.

She *was* seeing correctly.

The bed was empty. Feeling a gust of wind, Emily turned. The window was wide open. No *wonder* it was so cold in the room.

The window was wide open. And Jessie was gone.

Sneaked out. She probably climbed down the big old maple outside their window. But where did she go?

Feeling the bump under her pillow, Emily remembered the diary. She pulled it out and, yawning, carried it over to the desk and turned on the desk lamp.

It took a while for her sleep-filled eyes to focus on the tiny, precise handwriting. She kept thumbing backward through the days, not finding anything revealing.

Then a section caught her eye. It seemed to jump off the page because Jessie's handwriting suddenly changed, as if this particular passage had been written rapidly, heatedly.

Emily moved the desk lamp closer and started to

read. *Had a fight with Jolie,* the section began. *A big fight. I can't believe I trusted her. She is not a friend. She's the lowest. I hate her!*

Jolie. The name rang a bell with Emily. It was the name Jessie had mentioned the night of the shampoo incident.

Emily skimmed a few pages, then gasped as she started to read again. *They think I did it. They think I killed Jolie,* the diary said.

Killed Jolie?

Jolie isn't here anymore. They found us—just me and Jolie at the bottom of the slope. I told them I didn't do it. Jolie fell. It was an accident. It wasn't my fault. But Jolie is dead.

The handwriting became very sloppy at this point, the letters all jagged and run-together. *They think I killed Jolie. I guess I didn't handle it well at first. I couldn't answer their questions when the rest of our group found me next to her body. I guess I didn't make much sense. But it wasn't my fault! I kept saying that over and over. I could see that no one believed me. But I know the truth.*

I can tell that everyone thinks I killed her. I can tell by the way they look at me, by the way they whisper when I go past.

But you know what? I don't care. I really don't. I don't care what they think! Jolie is dead—nothing can change that. I have to go on with my life. I'm alive!

Emily slammed the book shut. She had read enough.

So that was the trouble Jessie had been in.

Jolie had died.

First, Jolie and Jessie had had a fight. And then Jolie was dead.

And everyone believed Jessie had killed her.

Was Jessie telling the truth in her diary? Did Jolie fall? Was it an accident? What really happened?

Was Jessie a murderer?

Her head spinning, Emily put the diary on the exact spot where she had found it.

I don't care what they think, Jessie had written.

Jolie was dead. And Jessie didn't care.

And where was Jessie now? Where had she run to?

Emily realized she was too tired to think straight. She climbed back into her bed and, seeing Jessie's scrawled words before her eyes, fell immediately into a troubled sleep.

"Pass the milk, please," Mr. Wallner said, scooting his stool up close to the counter. The whole family grabbed breakfast every morning around the kitchen counter, gulping down orange juice and milk, a quick bowl of cereal, or a couple slices of buttered toast. But it seemed different this morning, quieter without the clicking of Tiger's paws over the linoleum.

Emily, feeling as if she hadn't slept at all, thought of poor Tiger, lying lifeless out on the back stoop. She kept looking down to the floor, almost expecting to see him there, begging for crusts of toast. Since it was Saturday, everyone was still in pajamas and bathrobes, except for Emily, who had quickly pulled on jeans and a T-shirt.

Rich, looking very sleepy, kept giving Emily meaningful looks, which she didn't know how to interpret. Finally, she just stopped looking over at him.

What a weird kid, she thought. What a sad, weird kid.

"How are you feeling this morning, Em?" Mrs. Wallner asked, gripping her coffee cup tightly as if it might escape from her if she let go.

"I don't know. Okay, I guess," Emily answered.

"I know," Mrs. Wallner said cheerily, "why don't you and I spend the day together. We can go shopping and then have lunch like real ladies and—"

"Sorry, Mom. I'm going over to Kathy's. Then we're going to school. There's a special computer lab at school this morning, and—"

"On Saturday?" Mr. Wallner interrupted.

"Yeah. We get to try some new word-processing program. So Kathy and I thought we'd—"

"Morning, everyone." Jessie entered the kitchen quietly and climbed up onto the empty stool on the end, a pleasant smile on her face. "Pass the orange juice, please."

I wonder when she got in, Emily thought. Emily had been awakened by a garbage truck on the street at seven, and Jessie still hadn't returned to the room.

She was out all night, and look how perky she looks, Emily thought, staring as Jessie gulped down a tall glass of juice. I guess I underestimated Jessie's acting ability, Emily thought.

"You look very pretty today," Mrs. Wallner said to Jessie.

"Really? Thanks, I didn't sleep very well last night," Jessie said.

She's a good actress. And a good liar, Emily thought.

No one was talking about Tiger, Emily realized.

No one wanted to talk about the fact that a murder had been committed in this very kitchen the night before.

Maybe I'll tell everyone that Jessie sneaked out and was gone all night, Emily thought. Maybe I'll let them know what a sneak Jessie is.

But she didn't have the strength for a screaming confrontation this morning. She decided to save this little secret, save it for a time she really needed it.

"Maybe I'll help you clean the garage out this morning," Jessie said enthusiastically to her dad.

"Great!" he replied, his mouth full of cornflakes. "Too bad you won't be here, Emily," he said, leaning over the counter to see her better. "Then the whole family could pitch in. I like family activities."

Some family, Emily thought glumly.

A murder was committed here last night, and everyone's acting as if this is just another normal day.

She glanced at her watch. "Oh. I'm going to be late." She hopped down off the stool and hurried up to her room to get her backpack and her down jacket.

"Where are you going so early?" Nancy called, just coming down to breakfast.

"Out of here!" Emily shouted, slamming the door behind her.

When she picked up Kathy, she was still feeling really down. "What's your problem?" Kathy asked, noticing it immediately.

"If I tell you, you won't believe it," Emily told her friend bitterly.

"Wow," Kathy said. "What did your stepsister do this time?"

By the time they got to the computer lab in school, Emily had told her the whole story. She was reluctant at first. Why should Kathy have to hear the whole horrible tale? But it felt good to unburden herself—and it felt good to get some sympathy and understanding for a change.

"You poor thing," Kathy said as they found places at the long table in the lab. "If I had a wacko stepsister like that, I don't know *what* I'd do. Run away, probably."

"Well, I'm not running away," Emily said, pulling off her jacket. "I was there first."

She sighed loudly and plopped down in the chair. As the instructor entered the room, she pulled her backpack up onto the table and unzipped it.

She started to reach into the backpack—stopped—and screamed.

"Emily—what on earth!" Kathy cried.

Emily couldn't answer. Instead, her hand trembling, she pulled open the backpack.

"Oh, no. I don't believe it," Kathy groaned.

Someone had stuffed Tiger's corpse into the backpack.

chapter

11

The Silent Treatment

"No. We've barely said a word to each other in three days," Emily said into the phone in a low voice. "No, it isn't silly, Josh. She's crazy. She really is. And she's evil. She could do anything.

"I think I hear her coming up the stairs," Emily whispered, huddled over the phone on her desk. "Are you coming over later? Good. Bye."

She hung up just as Jessie walked into the room.

Her arms loaded down with books and papers, Jessie didn't glance at Emily, but walked straight to the back of the room and dropped everything onto the white counter that served as her desk. She sat down, humming very quietly to herself, and began sorting through the papers.

Emily didn't turn around. As she had been doing ever since Saturday morning, she ignored Jessie entirely. She opened her government textbook and sifted through it until she found the chapter she had to read.

She read a few minutes, then stopped. It was impossible to concentrate. The silence in the room was overwhelming.

How long can we go on like this? she wondered, sneaking a peek at Jessie, who was writing furiously in a notebook.

Sooner or later, Emily figured, the silent tension would lead to some kind of explosion. And of course, Emily thought bitterly, everyone would side with Jessie, as usual.

"Girls—come down for dinner!" Emily's mother shouted, her voice making Emily nearly jump out of the desk chair.

Chill out, girl, she warned herself. Or else Jessie's going to win this battle of nerves without even trying.

Jessie brushed past Emily, her nose in the air, as they left the bedroom. The aroma of roast lamb, Emily's favorite, drifted up the stairs. But Emily didn't care. She wasn't very hungry.

As Emily took her seat next to Nancy, she saw that Rich's cheek was cut, and he had a black eye. "What happened to you?" she blurted out.

Rich looked away, embarrassed. "Nothing."

"He got into a fight after school," Mr. Wallner said through clenched teeth.

"It was nothing," Rich repeated.

"A black eye and three stitches," Mr. Wallner grumbled.

"Really, Hugh. Let's talk about it later," Mrs. Wallner said, a forced smile on her face. "We should talk about more pleasant things at the dinner table. What did *you* do today?" she asked, turning to Nancy.

"Oh. The usual."

"Fascinating!" Mr. Wallner grumbled, chewing enthusiastically.

They ate in silence for a while. "I made all your favorites tonight," Mrs. Wallner said, smiling across the table at Emily.

"And it's all delicious," Emily said, even though she could barely taste any of it. Down the table from her, Rich and Jessie were having a private, almost-whispered conversation.

"Hey, Jessie," Mr. Wallner interrupted them. "Did I hear you talking on the phone late last night?"

"No. Wasn't me," Jessie said, looking surprised by the question.

Emily knew she was lying. Jessie made whispered, secretive late-night phone calls just about every night. She always waited until she thought Emily was asleep, then pulled the desk phone down to the floor and made her calls in the corner. She had also sneaked out the window in the middle of the night again two nights before, reappearing just before breakfast time.

"I had indigestion, so I had to get up," Mr. Wallner told Jessie. "I could've sworn I heard you on the phone."

"No. Must've been mice or something," Jessie lied.

Mrs. Wallner served baked apples for dessert. Emily ate less than half of hers, then asked to be excused. "I've got tons of homework," she explained.

"Tell me about it," Nancy grumbled.

"Josh is coming over later. Call me down if I don't hear the bell," Emily said, and went upstairs to try to concentrate on the chapter in her government text-book.

A short while later she thought she heard the front door slam. Was it Josh? No one called her down, so she continued to read.

She heard voices.

It *did* sound like Josh.

She closed the book and walked quietly to the stairs. She could see him in the hallway below. He was standing very close to Jessie, leaning with one hand against the closet door. They were talking animatedly, laughing together.

How cozy, Emily thought, feeling the anger grow inside her.

What does Jessie think she's doing?

What does *Josh* think he's doing?

She bounded down the stairs, deliberately making a lot of noise so they'd know she was coming. She stepped into the hallway, her eyes on Josh.

"Oh, hi, Emily," he said, sounding a little bit as if he hadn't expected her to be there. The anger must have been evident on her face, for he suddenly blushed and held up his book bag. "I've brought my books," he said. "Where do you want to study?"

"Let's get out of here," Emily said, not looking at Jessie but stepping in front of her to open the coat closet. "It's too crowded in this house to study."

Jessie turned angrily and started up the stairs. "See you, Josh," she called back.

"Yeah. Later," Josh said, standing back to give Emily room in the narrow hallway to pull on her down coat. "Wow," he said, tugging on a strand of his black, curly hair, as Emily pushed past him and opened the front door.

"What's that supposed to mean?" she asked curtly, still wondering why he and Jessie were suddenly so chummy.

"Just 'wow,'" he said, pulling the door closed after them. "You don't have to jump down my throat, you know. Just because you're mad at your stepsister, you don't have to take it out on me."

"I'm not mad at my stepsister," Emily corrected him. "I'm *terrified* of my stepsister. How many times do I have to tell you? I think she's totally deranged."

The air outside was cold and heavy. There was no moon in the gray-pink night sky. It felt like snow. Emily's sneakers crunched over the hard ground.

"She doesn't seem so bad," Josh said, struggling to catch up to her. "I can't believe she'd really do all those terrible things."

"Stop defending Jessie," Emily said sharply, spinning around to face him. "Why do you keep defending her?"

"I'm not," he said, surprised by her anger.

She looked up at the house. There was a shadow in the upstairs window, her bedroom window. It was Jessie, she realized. Jessie was watching them.

"Why is she spying on us?" Emily asked aloud without realizing it.

Jessie's diary flashed into her mind. She thought about it often. Sometimes Jessie's written words came back to her without warning:

THE STEPSISTER

They think I killed Jolie, **and** *I don't care what they think!*

She reached out and grabbed Josh's arm. Leaning against him, she struggled to catch her breath.

"What's wrong?" Josh asked.

She couldn't answer. How could she explain to him that, watching Jessie stare at them from the bedroom window, a dark shadow against the pale yellow lamplight, she was suddenly overcome with fear—fear for her life!

chapter
12

Up in Smoke

"**W**hat *is* this stuff?" Emily held up her fork and examined it, making a disgusted face.

"I don't know." Kathy, sitting across the table from her, shrugged. "It's too yellow to be macaroni and cheese."

"I've never seen this color before," Emily said, dropping her fork into the bright yellow puddle on her plate.

Kathy shoved her lunch tray away. "I've had enough." She pushed her chair back, stood up, and stretched. The lunchroom was emptying out quickly. Everyone was probably in a hurry to get away from the yellow substance in case it was radioactive!

"Later," Kathy said. "I see Lisa Blume over there. I've got to talk to her about our math test." She gave Emily a little wave and, balancing her tray in one hand, hurried off across the large, fluorescent-lit room.

Emily sighed and picked up her fork. She poked at her food for a few seconds, thinking about Josh, and then became aware that someone was standing beside her.

"Oh. Hi." She looked up to see Jessie's friend Krysta. Emily blinked a few times. Krysta was wearing the brightest, most garish Day-Glo orange blouse Emily had ever seen. With her brown corduroy slacks and that bright orange top, she looks like a Popsicle, Emily thought.

"You spilled something," Krysta said, pointing.

"What?"

"You spilled something on your shirt."

Emily looked down. "Oh, I don't believe it!" she exclaimed angrily. She had spilled a blob of the yellow macaroni-type substance on the front of her new pink shirt. She grabbed a napkin off her tray and tried dabbing at the spot, but that just buried it deeper into the fabric.

"Better get some cold water," Krysta said, frowning and shifting her weight. She sat down on the table edge and leaned toward Emily. "I just wanted to . . . uh . . . say something to you. I mean, ask you something, I guess." Her normally bland expression turned serious.

Uh-oh, Emily thought. What now?

"I'd better take care of this spot," Emily said, starting to get up.

"It'll only take a second," Krysta said, not moving from her position on the table. "I just wanted to know why you're being so terrible to Jessie."

"Huh?" Krysta's question caught Emily completely by surprise.

"Jessie is very upset," Krysta said. "Why are you being so awful to her?"

Emily started to sputter something, but no words came out.

"I know it's none of my business, but Jessie is my friend," Krysta continued. "Why don't you give her a break? She's not a bad kid, once you get to know her."

What do *you* know about her? Emily wanted to ask.

Do you know that she probably murdered her *last* best friend?

She stared up at Krysta, still too shocked to move or respond.

What horrible lies has Jessie been telling her? Emily wondered.

Jessie was such a good liar. All she had to do was widen those big blue eyes and smile her angelic smile, and everyone believed anything she told them. What had she made up about Emily? Whatever the lies were, Krysta was sure to spread them all over school. The two of them were the perfect team, Emily thought bitterly. A liar and a gossip.

She pushed herself to her feet, turned, and, leaving her tray on the table, shook her head at Krysta, as if to say she wouldn't dignify Krysta's questions with an answer. Then she started jogging toward the wide double doors.

"Hey, Emily—" Krysta yelled after her.

A few kids looked up to see what the fuss was about.

But Emily hurried on, without looking back. She stepped into the hall and turned toward the girls' room, which was at the end of the corridor across from the gym. "Hey, Em—" someone called, but Emily pretended she didn't hear.

As she neared her destination, Nancy came around the corner, looking troubled, a stack of books and notebooks in her arms. "Did the bell ring yet?" she asked Emily, not stopping.

"Not yet," Emily said. "Are you—"

"You spilled something on your shirt." Nancy was past her now, picking up speed.

"I know," Emily called after her. "I'm going to wash it off."

Nancy doesn't look good, Emily thought. She's working too hard. She's worrying about her schoolwork too much: And about her social life. She's never had trouble finding boys before. I don't know why she's so concerned that she isn't going with anyone now.

She started to pull open the girls' room door and bumped into Jessie, who was on her way out.

What's going on? Emily thought. Can't I go anywhere without bumping into my whole family?

"I can't take this anymore," Jessie said, her features set in a grim expression. She stopped in the doorway, holding it open with her shoulder, blocking Emily's way.

"What are you talking about?" Emily asked coldly.

"I can't take this silent treatment."

"Jessie—do we have to talk about this now? Can't I go into the bathroom without having a major confrontation?" She looked at her watch. "Give me a break. The bell is going to ring in two minutes."

"Why are you doing this to me?" Jessie asked. Her expression was hard, like stone. But her eyes were red-rimmed. She looked as if she were about to cry.

What an actress, Emily thought.

Doesn't she know I can see right through her phony theatrics?

"I'm not doing anything to you," Emily said impatiently. "Please. Go away."

"Answer my question. Why are you doing it?" Jessie said, not budging. Her voice trembled. Her whole body started to shake. "Why are you trying to ruin my life?"

"I'm not doing it. *You* are!" Emily said, starting to lose her cool. "How *dare* you try to turn things around! Don't you think I know all the horrible things you've done to me? Don't you think I know it's been *you* all along?"

"Me! What are you *talking* about?" Jessie cried loudly. "You're crazy!"

"I don't think *you* should be calling anyone crazy," Emily said heatedly. "I'm not the one who sees a shrink twice a week!"

She regretted saying it immediately. It had just slipped out.

But so what?

Why should she be careful about what she said to Jessie?

Jessie's eyes grew wide. Tears rolled down her pale cheeks. She opened her mouth to say something, changed her mind, and pushed past Emily, running full speed, her shoes clicking against the hard floor.

Emily breathed a loud sigh of relief and hurried into the bathroom, grateful there were no other family members inside. Her eyes quickly surveyed the large, black-and-white-tiled room, the row of sinks to her left, the stalls to her right, a painted-over window against the far wall. No one here.

Someone had left the water running in the first sink. Emily walked over and turned it off. As usual the bathroom was a mess. The sink was clogged with paper towels. And there were crumpled paper towels all over the floor.

She walked to the next sink, turned on the cold water, and dabbed at the spot on her shirt with a clean paper towel. She realized she was still breathing hard, still upset by her encounter with her stepsister.

First Krysta. Then Jessie.

What was the point of this campaign they were mounting?

What had Jessie and Krysta cooked up between them? What were they trying to prove, anyway?

Was Jessie trying to prove for some reason that Emily was some sort of horrible person? What was the point of that? Was it Jessie's way of denying the truth—that *she* was crazy, that *she* was the horrible one?

Emily dabbed at the spot on her shirt. She couldn't tell if the stain had come out or not. Now she had a dark, wet circle on her chest.

Oh, great, she thought wearily. That's really going to look great in English class next period.

Feeling sorry for herself, wishing the school day

were over so she could get outside, away from everyone, and breathe some fresh air, Emily entered the middle stall, locking the door behind her.

Sitting down, she let her mind wander. She tried to think of something pleasant, something nice, to take her mind off Jessie. She started to think about Josh, but then she pictured him leaning so close to Jessie, talking and laughing with her so cozily. "Yuck!" she said aloud.

She heard someone come into the girls' room. Heard shoes scraping against the tile floor. Heard water running into the sink.

The water stopped. Someone coughed. Then the shoes scuffed against the floor. The door opened and closed. The bathroom was empty again.

A few seconds later Emily smelled smoke.

She got up quickly and hurried out of the stall. Her heart was pounding.

The room was filling with white smoke.

Where was it coming from?

Emily held her breath. The wastebasket. Flames leapt from the wastebasket at the end of the stalls.

So much smoke, she thought, for a wastebasket fire.

Coughing, her eyes starting to tear, she ran over to see if she could smother the flames. But the flames were leaping high from the can, too high to get near enough to move the can.

And then suddenly the paper on the floor caught fire. And now the flames were leaping up to the wooden moldings on the walls.

I've got to get out of here, Emily thought, surprised by how frightened she felt. I've got to set off the alarm.

The fire started to spread over the wooden doors of the stalls.

Emily ran to the door leading to the hall and shoved.

"Hey—what's going on?"

The door seemed to be stuck.

"Hey!"

She shoved again, jamming her shoulder hard against the door.

But it didn't budge.

It *couldn't* be stuck.

Was someone standing on the other side, holding it closed?

Don't get paranoid, Emily, she thought.

She coughed again. The smoke was burning her throat.

Don't get paranoid? While Emily was in the stall, someone had come in and set the wastebasket on fire!

Jessie?

She tried the door again. It didn't move.

Trying desperately to hold her breath, she lowered her head and ran past the flames to the little window in the back of the bathroom. Her eyes closed, she grabbed the window frame and tugged.

No.

Come on. Come on. Move.

No.

She tugged harder. The window wouldn't raise.

Choking on the acrid smoke, she opened her eyes and saw the problem. The window frame had recently been painted. The window was painted shut.

"No! Help! Somebody—help!"

The smoke had turned black. It seemed to billow up in all directions.

She ran through the flames to the door at the front and heaved herself against it with all her might.

The door wouldn't move.

"I'm going to die in here," she said aloud.

chapter

13

*H*er throat burned. Her eyes burned. She couldn't catch her breath.

She ran to the nearest sink and turned on both faucets, splashing her face with water.

It didn't help.

It wouldn't help at all, she realized.

But what if she filled the wastebasket with water and then used it to douse the flames?

Yes. That might work. But where was the wastebasket? The smoke had formed a swirling, black curtain. She couldn't even see the wastebasket.

I—I can't breathe, she thought.

I'm going to suffocate.

Uttering a loud sob, she pounded on the door with her fists.

"Help me! Please—help me!"

No reply.

The bell must have rung. Everyone must have gone upstairs to class. The downstairs hallway would be deserted by now.

"Help me! Please—help me!"

She tried to pound on the door, but she could feel herself weakening. Her arms felt so heavy, she could barely lift them.

She choked, gasping for breath.

If only I could catch up with my breathing. . . .

She couldn't see.

The flames were so hot now. So high . . . so close. . . .

And then she heard someone struggling with the door. "It's my imagination." Did she say that aloud, or did she just think it?

Her mind was becoming a cloud, as dark and swirling as the smoke. She felt light, as light as a flame.

The door was pulled open.

She wanted to run to it, but she was floating now, floating in the dark, dark air.

"Is anyone in there? Oh, my God—Emily!"

Emily floated, so warm, so unbearably warm.

"If only I could breathe . . ."

Strong arms pulled her away. She floated through the dark curtain of smoke. She floated to the door.

"Emily—are you okay?"

Choking and sputtering, she staggered out into the cool, cool hall. She tried to take deep breaths but her heart was pounding too hard.

"Emily, just sit down on the floor." Mrs. Hoffler, the teacher, looked very worried. "I've got to sound the alarm."

Emily leaned against a column, pressing her face against the cool concrete. I'm going to be okay. I'm going to stop choking. I'm going to breathe again. And I'll be okay.

She saw Mrs. Hoffler open the glass door in the alarm and pull the lever. A bell went off somewhere above her head.

I'm going to be okay.

"Mrs. Hoffler!" Emily called. The teacher was tall and very skinny. The kids called her Mrs. Stork behind her back.

"Mrs. Hoffler! I'm going to be okay!"

The teacher hurried to Emily's side. "Yes. Yes, you are," she said, looking very relieved.

Flames leapt out from under the bathroom door.

"We've got to get out of here," Mrs. Hoffler said, shouting over the alarm. "Think you can walk?"

"Sure," Emily said. She took a step away from the column, then another. So dizzy. So light-headed.

She fell to her knees. "Ouch."

"Let me help you," Mrs. Hoffler said. "You must have breathed in a lot of smoke." She pulled Emily to her feet and, putting a strong arm around her waist, guided her to the door. "This doorstop was stuck under the door," she said, holding up the wooden triangle, then tossing it away. "It's usually under the hallway door right here. How on earth did it get stuck in the bathroom door?"

They reached the stairway leading to the first floor. "Emily, how did the fire start?" the teacher asked.

"I don't know," Emily said, still struggling to catch her breath

I'll bet Jessie knows, Emily thought angrily. Jessie was the only one who knew I was in that bathroom.

Her legs felt so heavy going up the stairs. Mrs. Hoffler practically had to drag her.

Emily stopped at the top step, leaning heavily against the tall teacher, one hand refusing to let go of the railing. "I—I can't breathe!" she cried suddenly, her voice so terror-filled, she didn't recognize it.

"You'll feel better in the cold air," Mrs. Hoffler said, pushing open the heavy door and guiding Emily outside.

The cold air was a shock. Emily breathed deeply. She was shaking all over, but it didn't matter.

I'm alive, she thought. I'm breathing.

The dark curtain seemed to lift from her eyes. The world became clear again. Colors returned.

What were the sounds that grew louder and louder?

It was the laughter and loud voices of Shadyside students. Leaning against Mrs. Hoffler, Emily realized for the first time that they weren't alone out here on the sidewalk, out here in the gray afternoon cold. Everyone was here. Everyone had been evacuated from the building. Everyone was standing out here, coatless, jumping up and down to keep warm.

Emily heard sirens in the distance. The fire trucks must be on their way, she thought.

And then Nancy was standing in front of her. "Oh, Nancy!" Emily cried emotionally and, to her surprise, collapsed into Nancy's arms.

"Em—what's wrong?" Nancy cried, catching Emily before she fell.

"She was trapped in the bathroom, where the fire started," Mrs. Hoffler explained quickly.

"Oh, no!" Nancy's normally pale skin became flour white. "Are you okay?"

"I think so," Emily said.

"Is she in shock or anything?" Nancy asked Mrs. Hoffler.

"Why don't you ask *me?*" Emily demanded, angry for some reason. "Why ask *her?*"

"No, I guess not," Nancy said, a little color returning to her cheeks. "She sounds like herself." She grinned at Emily, a grin of sheer relief.

Everyone cheered as the fire trucks pulled right up onto the grass of the school grounds and serious-faced firemen leapt off and began pulling out a long, gray hose.

"It was scary," Emily told her sister, hugging herself to keep warm.

"I'm going to take Emily home," Nancy told Mrs. Hoffler. "Unless you think she has to go to the hospital or something."

"No," Emily said. "I mean, I'm fine. Really." She heard the sound of breaking glass. The firemen must be using axes, she thought. Everything was clear now, clear and bright. She stared at the smiling, laughing faces of the kids huddled in groups all over the school grounds, delighted to have this excuse to be out of school.

They don't know what it's like, she thought. They don't know how frightening fire is. "Take me home—please," she told Nancy.

"I guess it's all right," Mrs. Hoffler said. Someone was calling her. "Go ahead." She turned and headed toward the insistent voice.

"Thank you, Mrs. Hoffler!" Emily shouted. She wasn't sure the teacher had heard her. It was an inadequate thank-you for saving her life, anyway, Emily realized. She decided to bring Mrs. Hoffler a present—flowers maybe—tomorrow.

A few minutes later Emily slid into the passenger seat of the small Corsica Nancy drove to school. Nancy started the engine. Emily closed the door and rested her head on the seatback, closing her eyes.

"Are you sure you're okay?" Nancy asked. The car started on the second try.

"Yeah. I guess."

"You know, there's an ambulance here. It came after the fire trucks. Maybe someone should look at you. You know, examine your lungs or something."

"No, Nancy. Please. I'm okay. Let's just go home. I'll lie down for a bit at home. Okay?"

Nancy backed out of the parking spot and carefully headed out of the student parking lot and onto Park Drive. Behind them, kids were cheering for some reason. Maybe the fire had spread over the entire building. Emily didn't turn around to see.

"So where were you? In the bathroom?" Nancy asked, speaking quickly, her voice tight.

"Yes. Downstairs. You know. Across from the gym."

"And a fire started?" Nancy sounded very confused.

"It didn't start. Somebody started it," Emily said, opening her eyes and sitting up.

"Huh?"

"Nancy, look out!"

Nancy had driven through a Stop sign and had nearly hit an oncoming car. The driver shouted something out his window and shook his fist.

"Sorry," Nancy called out meekly. She turned to Emily. "What did you say? Why didn't you get out of the bathroom? Why didn't you go out the window or something?"

"The window was painted shut," Emily explained. "Besides, it was a basement window. You know. Underground. I would've had to climb up to—"

"But why didn't you go out the door?" Nancy asked, putting both hands high on the steering wheel, trying to concentrate on her driving even though she was more interested in getting Emily's story.

"It was jammed. Somebody jammed it shut with the doorstop from the hallway door."

"I don't believe it!" Nancy exclaimed, shaking her head.

"Believe it," Emily told her bitterly.

They turned onto Fear Street. A few more blocks and they'd be home.

"Someone came into the bathroom. I didn't see who it was. And they started the fire," Emily explained.

"You mean someone deliberately tried to—"

"Someone deliberately started the fire. And then jammed the door shut. I know it," Emily said, surprised at how calmly she could say those words.

"Sometimes kids start fires in wastebaskets for no reason. Just messing around. You know. And I guess the doorstop could have gotten stuck accidentally."

"I don't think it was an accident," Emily said, her voice still calm, still cool. "I think it was Jessie. And I think she knew what she was doing."

Nancy pulled the car up the drive and slammed on the brakes. Neither girl moved to get out of the car.

Nancy turned in the driver's seat to face her sister. "That's a serious accusation."

"It was a serious fire," Emily said, crossing her arms over her chest, looking straight ahead through the windshield. "Jessie tried to kill me. I know it."

"But how would she know you were in that bathroom?"

"I ran into her coming out. She started yelling at me, accusing me of being terrible to her."

"What?"

"You heard me. She ran off, doing this phony crying routine. She didn't fool me for a second. But, of course, I had no way of knowing she planned to come back and murder me."

"This is dreadful," Nancy said, her voice cracking. She looked as if she might cry. She took Emily's hand in both of hers and squeezed it tightly. "And you really think that Jessie started the fire?"

"I know she did."

"But you have no proof," Nancy said.

"Proof?" Emily jerked her hand out of Nancy's. "What proof do I need? My dead body?"

Emily realized she shouldn't be yelling at her sister. "I'm sorry. I guess I'm more upset than I thought. I mean, I almost *died* in there, Nancy. Jessie almost got her wish."

Nancy didn't say anything. She stared down at the steering wheel, seemingly lost in thought.

"You do believe me, don't you?" Emily asked. "About Jessie?"

Nancy thought for a long moment. Then she turned to her sister. "Yes. Yes, I do. From what you told me about Jessie's diary, and from the little bit that Mom let slip about her, I think Jessie is definitely dangerous. I believe you, Em."

"So what are we going to do?" Emily asked.

"I'm going to help you get the proof you need so we can convince Mom and Hugh," Nancy said.

"You mean—"

"From now on, I'm going to keep my eye on Jessie. I'm going to make it my business to know every move Jessie makes. I'm going to stick to her like glue. I want you to just lay off, to just cool it. Just avoid her as much as you can. Let me handle this."

"But, Nancy—"

"She hasn't given me any trouble—right? So she won't suspect that I'm going to be the one to expose her. When I have the proof we need, then you and I will sit down quietly with Mom and Hugh and tell them everything."

Emily leaned her head back against the car seat. She still felt trembly all over. But she also felt relieved that Nancy believed her, that Nancy was going to help her.

"Come on. Let's go inside." Nancy pushed open the door and climbed out of the car. She came around to the other side and held the door open for Emily.

"How do you feel?" She helped Emily up from the low car seat.

"Better. Really. You don't have to help me up. I'm just a little jumpy, that's all."

Nancy took her arm and led her up the flagstone walk to the front door. "It's not going to be easy," Emily said, surprised at how dizzy she still felt.

"What isn't?"

"Convincing Mom and Hugh that their golden girl has been trying to kill me."

"Just let me worry about that," Nancy said, unlocking the door and following Emily into the house. She was about to go make Emily some hot tea when the door burst open and Jessie came rushing in.

"Emily—I heard what happened!" Jessie cried, her face filled with emotion. She lunged across the room and threw her arms around Emily, drawing her into a tight hug. "Oh, Emily—are you okay? Are you okay?"

She pressed her face against Emily's and wouldn't let go. Her face was burning hot.

"Oh, let's be friends—okay?" Jessie cried, her arms still around Emily. "Let's start all over again. Okay? Please?"

Emily was too shaken to speak.

Despite the heat radiating off Jessie, Jessie's impassioned hug made Emily feel cold all over.

Colder than she had ever felt.

Struggling to free herself from Jessie's emotional grip, Emily realized that she had never been so afraid in her life.

chapter

14

Rocking—and Rolling

Nancy lifted her foot off the brake and eased the car forward a few feet, then quickly braked again. "We'll never get there," Emily whined. "The concert will be over, and we'll still be trying to get into the parking lot."

"I can't even see Vets Auditorium from here!" Jessie complained.

"Give me a break," Nancy said softly, waiting for the car in front of her to move. "We still have half an hour. That should be enough time. Besides, there's always a warm-up band."

"But the warm-up band is the Deltoids," Emily said, rolling down her window and trying to get some fresh air, but inhaling only car exhaust fumes. "Kathy saw them at a little club the last time they were in Waynesbridge, and she said they were awesome."

"Awesome?" Jessie laughed. "Emily, I never knew you to be such a *teenager!*"

Emily didn't return the laugh. And she didn't turn around to acknowledge her stepsister's presence in the back seat.

Ever since the fire, Jessie had been extra nice to Emily. Much *too* nice, in Emily's opinion. She didn't want Jessie helping out with her chores and offering to run errands for her.

She wanted Jessie to leave her alone.

Emily knew that Jessie had tried to kill her. She was just waiting until Nancy had gotten the proof they needed. Then they would show Hugh and her mother. Then they would make sure that Jessie got the treatment she needed. And make sure that Jessie was safely out of Emily's life.

In the meantime Emily had been trying to stay as far away from Jessie as possible. Having to share the same car with her made Emily very nervous.

She hadn't wanted Jessie to come to the rock concert with them. Emily had three tickets to the huge auditorium in Waynesbridge, the next town. One for herself, one for Nancy, and one for Josh. But at the last minute, Josh had had to help out at his father's store.

"Who should I invite?" Emily had asked Nancy. She didn't know that Jessie was eavesdropping.

"Oh, please, please, please," Jessie started to beg. "Let me come with you. I'll even pay you for the ticket."

Emily looked at Nancy, as if to say, Get me out of this fix. I don't want to give the ticket to Jessie.

Nancy just shrugged.

Jessie pleaded some more.

Emily was about to tell Jessie "no way" when her mother entered the room. "Why is Jessie down on her knees begging like that?" she asked.

Emily had to tell her. "Well, of *course* Jessie can go," Mrs. Wallner said, oblivious to the looks Emily was giving her.

Jessie jumped up and down happily.

"Of course," Emily said, trying to sound gracious about it, even though she was furious. The concert was ruined for her. Maybe I'll just get sick and skip it, she thought.

Why couldn't her mother mind her own business? And why was she always sticking up for Jessie, always on Jessie's side? Was she really blind to everything that Jessie was doing?

The answer to that question, Emily knew, was yes.

So here they were, just outside the Vets Auditorium parking lot on a Saturday night, creeping forward an inch at a time, nervously glancing at their watches, wondering if they'd get inside before the concert started.

"Oh, turn up the radio. I love this song!" Jessie cried, leaning over into the front, trying to reach the radio.

"Ugh." Nancy made a face. "How can you listen to that? He has such a whiny voice. He sings everything through his nose."

"I think that's sexy," Jessie said.

Nancy turned up the radio until the car windows vibrated. At least it drowns out all the honking horns, Emily thought.

A white Honda Civic roared past them, at least six

boys crammed in like sardines. "Where do they think they're going? They're trying to ditch ahead of everyone," Nancy said angrily.

"No one will let them back in line," Jessie said. "Did you see the driver? He was kinda cute."

"Now who's being the teenager?" Emily said, laughing.

"Well, I *am* a teenager," Jessie replied. "What's wrong with acting like one?"

"Hey—we're moving now!" Nancy exclaimed. She eased the car forward two entire car lengths.

"Only twenty minutes until eight," Jessie said, looking at her watch for the two thousandth time.

"They never start on time," Emily said.

They pulled the car into a parking place at about eight-fifteen. It was a warm, windless night, so they pulled off their down jackets and locked them in the car. Then all three of them went tearing at full speed in their jeans and sweatshirts across the vast, nearly filled parking lot.

"I don't hear any music," Jessie said as they crowded through the enormous marble lobby of the old theater and made their way up to the row of ticket-takers at the theater entrance.

"It probably won't start for another hour," Nancy said, shouting over the laughter and loud voices. "These bands never show up on time. And then they warm up for two hours."

The uniformed ticket-taker, a thin-faced young man with a complexion that resembled the surface of the moon, reached a hand up to Emily for the tickets, but his gaze was toward the parking lot. "You're about the last ones," he said, shaking his head. He tore the three tickets in half, then glanced down at them. "Stairway to your left. All the way to the top."

"Top?" Emily repeated, looking at her stubs.

"Yeah. You're way up on top. Hope you don't get a nosebleed!" he said, and laughed a high-pitched laugh, as if he'd never made that joke before.

Emily followed Nancy and Jessie into the auditorium and looked to the stage. The lights were up, but the stage was bare, except for a few roadies in jeans and T-shirts, scrambling about, fiddling with the microphones and giant amps.

"Good. We haven't missed anything," Emily said.

"Told you," Nancy called back. She stopped at the bottom step to the balcony and looked up. It looked like a steep, dark, concrete mountain.

"That guy wasn't kidding about nosebleeds!" Jessie complained.

They started up the stairs. It actually feels good to climb after being cooped up in the car, Emily thought.

A short while later they stepped out into the balcony and looked around. The steep aisle was empty. Everyone was seated, waiting for the show to start. "We still have more to climb," Jessie said, pointing up. They had come out in the middle of the top balcony. A narrow stairway led up to the top seats.

"Finally!" Jessie cried, out of breath, when they found their row and slid into their seats. "Hey, look— I can almost see the stage from up here!"

All she does is complain, Emily thought. Nobody asked her to come, after all.

"Hey, we're not in the last row," Nancy said,

turning to look behind them. "There are three more rows and— Hey, Carla! Carla!" Nancy recognized someone from school. "Hey, I'll be right back." She climbed out of the row and went up to talk to her friend.

A few seconds later the warm-up band, the Deltoids, sauntered out and started to tune up. Emily suddenly realized she was dying of thirst and then saw a vendor on the lower balcony carrying a large basket of sodas on his head.

"I'm going to get a drink. Want anything?" Emily asked Jessie.

Jessie shook her head. Emily climbed over her and stepped out into the empty aisle. She looked for the soda vendor, spotted him about two miles down, and started to make her way down the steep, narrow steps.

She had only taken two or three steps when the Deltoids let loose with a loud piercing chord. The lights went out and the crowd exploded with cheers and clapping. Emily tried to figure out whether to continue down or turn around and go back up when someone shoved her—a hard deliberate shove high on her back—and she started to fall.

chapter
15

An Accident

"Oh!"

She tried to catch her balance, but she was falling forward and there was nothing to grab on to.

Her shoulder hit the concrete stair, sending pain up her arm like a powerful shock of electricity. She cried out again, and realized she was going to roll down all the stairs unless something—or someone—blocked her path.

"Ow!" Her head hit the concrete. She heard alarmed screams. Hands reached out for her from the seats on both sides. But they were too late to catch her or slow her fall.

"No!"

Looking up as she fell, she saw Jessie standing at the top of the empty aisle, staring down at her, hands on her hips, as if satisfied with a job well done.

"No! No! No!"

She banged her knee, rolled over again—and finally someone grabbed her, stopping her fall.

"Are you okay?" someone shouted over the loud music.

"Yeah, I guess," she managed to reply.

Whoever it was quickly disappeared to his seat.

Everything ached.

She tried to stand, but sank back onto her knees on the hard, cold floor of the aisle. From down below on the stage the twangs and squeals of the band seemed to bounce around inside her head and make her feel even dizzier.

She closed her eyes.

The whole fall must have lasted only two or three seconds.

When she opened them, Jessie was running down the stairs, with Nancy right behind her, looking very frightened.

"What happened?" Nancy called. "I was talking to Carla. Then I turned around and saw you falling. How did you fall like that?"

"I didn't fall. Somebody pushed me," Emily said, staring hard at Jessie.

Jessie leaned down and gently started to help Emily to her feet. "It must have been an accident," Jessie said. "No one would do that on purpose." She looked innocently into Emily's eyes. "You could have been killed," she said.

chapter
16

Jessie and Josh

*T*he weather finally turned cold, the kind of wet cold that clings to your clothes and makes your ears burn. The wind blew the trees, bending them back and shaking down the remaining brown leaves. The full moon disappeared behind a thick curtain of gray-pink clouds. It felt like snow.

Emily turned the corner onto Fear Street, walking quickly, rolling up her coat sleeve to check her watch. Ten-fifteen. Her breath, steamy and white, fogged the watch crystal.

She pulled the blue wool cap down tighter over her ears and began walking faster. The wind blew a stampede of crackling, brown leaves past her, and for a moment she felt as if she might be swept away with them, carried by the wind down this familiar street that was still frightening even though she knew every house, every empty lot, practically every tree.

Fear Street.

Some of her friends teased her about living on this street that held so many dark legends for the town of Shadyside. Emily had lived on Fear Street most of her life, since she was seven or eight, and hadn't witnessed any of the horrors her friends teased her about.

Sure, she had sometimes heard strange moans and howls coming from the woods late at night. But the Fear Street cemetery never held any particular horror for her. And she didn't really believe all the Fear Street stories about unsolved murders and mysterious disappearances, stories that sometimes even made it into the Shadyside newspaper.

Nevertheless, she picked up her pace as soon as she got to Fear Street, jogging along the side of the narrow, tree-lined road as it curved toward her house, her heart pounding just a little faster than usual, her eyes wide, alert to anything that moved.

She had been studying at Kathy's house, just a few blocks away on Hawthorne Drive, and had lost track of the time. Actually, she had deliberately lost track of the time, she realized. It was so nice to be at Kathy's, away from her own house, away from . . . Jessie.

How sad, Emily thought, not to be comfortable in your own home.

How . . . unbearable.

The wind shifted. The scuttling brown leaves were coming at her now. Her house came into view, dark against the deep red sky. "Couldn't someone at least turn on the porch light?" she asked aloud.

Doesn't anyone care about me anymore? she thought.

And then she stopped.

There was a blue car parked in the cul-de-sac around the corner from her house. Josh's Toyota.

That's strange, Emily thought, beginning to jog again. Why would he park so far from the house? He always pulls up the drive.

What is he doing here?

Her puzzlement gave way to happiness. What a nice surprise—Josh came to visit me, she thought. Josh wasn't the most spontaneous person in the world. It was a good sign that he had just decided to pop in unexpectedly.

Despite the cold that made her nose and cheeks feel numb, Emily was suddenly flooded with warm feelings. I'm so lucky, she thought. Josh is such a great guy. And he really seems to care about me.

She jogged past the cul-de-sac, eager to get to her house. The sky suddenly lost its color, fading from red to black. It was so dark now she could barely see the car, even though she was just a few yards beyond it.

But something caught her eye. A movement inside A flash of color against the fogged-up window.

Emily stopped. Someone was in the car.

"Josh?"

Her voice came out tiny. She was out of breath from jogging along the street.

She took a few steps toward the car.

Why would he be sitting by himself in there? Why hadn't he gone up to the house to wait where it was warm?

"Oh."

The window was steamed up, but she could suddenly see that he wasn't alone in there. Staring from the darkness of the curb, so close to the car yet feeling a million miles away, as if watching through a telescope, she could see that someone was in the front seat with him. It was hard to see clearly. But she saw enough. It was Jessie!

Josh had his arms wrapped around her. And they were frozen in a long, passionate kiss.

"Oh."

Emily stood in the drive staring into the steamed-up window.

She wasn't seeing things—was she? It *was* Jessie in there with Josh—right?

Yes.

She suddenly felt so heavy. So heavy she wanted to drop down onto the driveway. So heavy she wanted to sink through the asphalt and just keep sinking, sinking into the earth until she disappeared forever.

Jessie and Josh?

She wanted to scream. She wanted to pound on the car window. Tear open the door. Pull them both out into the cold.

But she felt so heavy, so weighed down, so paralyzed.

Somehow she started to run.

Before she even realized it, she was past the blue Toyota and running at full speed away from the car, away from the house, running into the wind, into the clattering leaves which blew up against her, brushing her legs, as if trying to push her back, back to the scene she didn't want to see.

Jessie and Josh?

Her dismay at seeing them locked together in that steamy embrace turned to fury.

Jessie was ruining her life in every way!

Jessie killed her dog, tried to kill her—and now she had taken Josh!

"Why is she doing this?" Emily asked herself. "Why does she hate me *so much?*"

She kept running into the wind, her face frozen, her eyes tearing, ducking her head, running without seeing where she was going, everything a dark blur, the only sound the scraping, scratching of the blowing, dead leaves.

I'm going back there, she thought, her heart pounding.

I'm going to confront her. I can't let her drive me out of my own house, out of my own *life*.

Is that what Jessie wanted? Did she want to have Emily's *life?*

Well, she's not getting it without a fight, Emily thought, her anger turning her around, forcing her back.

I'm through being the victim.

I'm ready to face her down. I want my own life back. I'm not going to let Jessie steal everything.

Walking fast, her mouth trailing white steam with every step, she rounded the curve toward her house. And saw that the car was gone.

Feeling a mixture of relief and disappointment, Emily ran up the drive, tore off her gloves, fumbled with frozen hands in her backpack until she found her house key, and let herself in through the front door.

Nancy was in the front hall. Startled by Emily

bursting in, she nearly dropped the glass of diet soda she was holding. "Oh—it's you," she said, recovering quickly. "Close the door. You're bringing the cold in with you. Look at you—you look frozen!" Nancy chattered nervously. "How come you—"

"Where are Josh and Jessie?" Emily demanded, breathing hard.

"What?"

"Josh and Jessie—where are they?" Emily leaned on the banister, trying to catch her breath.

"I don't know. I haven't seen them," Nancy said, confused. "What's your problem, anyway?"

"Is Jessie upstairs?" Emily asked, ignoring Nancy's question.

"No. I don't think she's back. She went over to Krysta's. At least, that's what she said. She won't be back till later."

"Krysta's?"

Jessie was such a liar.

She told them she was going to Krysta's, then spent the evening with Josh.

Kissing in the car.

Steaming up the windows with Emily's boyfriend.

"What's wrong with you? You're bright red," Nancy said. "Why are you acting so weird?"

Without answering, Emily turned and ran up the stairs. She couldn't explain it all to Nancy now. She knew if she started, she'd burst into tears.

She wanted to hold it all in, hold it in until Jessie got home.

The upstairs hallway was dark. Her eyes struggled to adjust. Everything looked red for a few seconds.

She blinked, waiting for everything to come into focus, then stopped at the door to her room.

The door was closed for some reason. She put her ear to the door and listened.

Someone was moving around in there.

What's going on? she thought.

Are Josh and Jessie in my bedroom?

She took a deep breath and pushed open the door.

chapter

17

Oh, Brother

"What are you doing in here?" Emily asked, her voice coming out shaky and high-pitched.

Rich looked up from her bed, startled. "Oh. Hi." His face turned bright red. He closed the book he had been reading, turned, and sat up.

Emily walked into the room. All of the lights were on. Rich had been lying on top of her covers, the bed still made.

"What are you doing in here?" she repeated, forcing her voice down, starting to feel a little calmer.

"I—I'm sorry," Rich stammered. He stood up awkwardly, dropped the book onto the rug, bent over to pick it up. "I was just . . . reading."

"But why?" Emily demanded, walking closer. She pulled off her coat and tossed it onto the desk chair.

"There were . . . uh . . . noises. In my room. I don't know. I guess I got scared." Rich looked very scared now. Is he really that frightened of me? she wondered. Or does he have some other reason to be scared?

"So I came in here," he said, edging toward the door. "It was quiet in here. I just wanted to read."

Emily couldn't decide whether to believe Rich or not. He certainly didn't look as if he were telling the truth. But, she realized, Rich always looked guilty. He always looked as if he had just done something wrong and knew he was about to be caught.

He was the most nervous boy she had ever known. He had been living with her in the same house for weeks now, and Emily realized she didn't know the first thing about him.

Except that he was shy and liked to read horror novels. And that he was constantly getting into trouble in school and had been caught shoplifting a cassette.

Beyond that, he was still a total stranger.

And now there he was, standing against the wall, his face still red, looking so guilty, so . . . frightened.

Emily found herself feeling sorry for the kid. "Do you want to stay and read a little longer?" she asked.

"No. No, thanks." He smiled at her. It was the first time she had ever seen him smile. "That's real nice of you." He seemed genuinely touched by her offer.

"Well . . ." She was beginning to feel as awkward as he looked.

"I'll go back to my room. The noises are probably gone. I shouldn't have gotten scared. It's just—it's just . . . Oh, well." He shrugged and disappeared out the door.

Weird kid, Emily thought.

As soon as he was gone, her anger returned.

She dropped down onto her bed. She saw the steamed-up Toyota again. Saw Josh and Jessie wrapped up in the front seat.

Where were they now? Where had they gone together?

Those nights that Jessie had sneaked out of the house—had she sneaked out to see Josh?

Suddenly Emily felt sick.

I can't spend another night in this room with her, she thought. She jumped to her feet.

I can't spend another minute in the same room with an enemy.

I'll sleep downstairs in the den, Emily thought.

Her heart was pounding. Her temples throbbed. She knew she wasn't thinking clearly. But she knew she had to get out of that room.

Without realizing it, she was pacing back and forth, her arms crossed tightly over her chest.

Jessie and Josh.

Jessie and Josh.

Jessie and Josh.

"Hey, Em—" Nancy poked her head into the room. "Everything okay? Why are you pacing back and forth like that?"

"I really don't want to talk right now," Emily said, not meaning to sound as harsh as she did.

"Well, excuuuuuuse me!" Nancy exclaimed with exaggerated outrage.

"I—I really need to be left alone," Emily said.

"Good night, Em." Nancy disappeared as quickly as she had appeared.

Emily paced a little more, thinking of Jessie and Josh. Then she walked over to the dresser and began searching for her flannel nightgown. It was chilly in the den. The flannel nightgown would keep her warm.

I'll take my pillow and a blanket, she thought. I'll be perfectly comfortable.

But she couldn't find the nightgown.

Maybe it's in one of Jessie's drawers, she thought.

She searched through Jessie's top drawer without success. Jessie's second drawer was jammed to the top with clothes. Searching quickly, Emily pulled up a pile of brightly colored scarves, all folded perfectly into squares.

Beneath the scarves was a knife.

A large kitchen knife.

The blade of the knife was covered with dried blood.

Emily knew at once what it was. It was the knife that had killed Tiger.

chapter
18

In Grave Condition

"A camping trip? I can't go on a camp-ing trip!" Nancy cried, dropping her soup spoon into her tomato soup. The splash sent a red splotch onto the place mat.

Everyone around the dinner table reacted to Mr. Wallner's suggestion with equal horror.

"I'm really busy this weekend," Jessie said.

"I have so much homework, I can't go anywhere!" Nancy cried.

Mr. Wallner smiled patiently, as if expecting this negative reaction. "It's just for the weekend." He looked over to Emily's mom, who smiled back at him.

"It'll be fun," she said.

"No, it won't," Rich said glumly. "I hate camping out."

"How do you know?" Mr. Wallner snapped, quick-ly losing his cool. "You've never done it. This is a beautiful spot. At least, it was when I was a boy."

"We're going to South Carolina just for a week-end?" Emily asked, still not believing it.

"It's too cold to camp up here," Mr. Wallner said, slurping his tomato soup.

"Hugh got a special bonus this week," Mrs. Wallner said proudly, as if he had won the Medal of Honor.

"But why do we have to go camping?" Nancy whined.

"Because we're all stir crazy," Mr. Wallner said, wiping his chin with a paper napkin. "Everyone is at everyone else's throat. We all have cabin fever, and winter hasn't really even begun yet."

"But why camping?" Rich asked, making a face.

"It'll be good for us to have to work together, outdoors on our own, as a family," Mr. Wallner said.

"We're going to fly all the way to South Carolina to do that?" Nancy asked, saying South Carolina as if it were on the moon.

"That's how eager Hugh is for us to start acting like a family," Emily's mother said, blowing on her soup spoon, then sipping carefully.

Boy, is *he* in for a major disappointment, Emily thought. She and Nancy were just waiting for the right moment to expose Jessie to the whole family. After showing the bloodstained knife to Nancy, Emily had hidden it in a safe place. Now she and Nancy were going to organize their evidence, get their story completely straight so that no one would doubt her accusations.

There's no way this family is ever going to act like a real family, Emily thought. Not until my psycho stepsister is out of here.

The argument over whether or not to go camping continued through the soup, through the tuna casserole and salad, and on into the banana-cream pie. By this time Jessie had completely turned around. She was now wildly in favor of the trip. "It'll be great fun. We'll be like a pioneer family," she said with great enthusiasm, looking across the table at Emily for some reason.

Uh-oh, thought Emily. What has she got in her sick, devious mind? Why has she changed her tune about this camping trip? And why is she looking at me like that, like a hungry shark closing in on a little minnow?

Jessie's smile filled her with dread.

"The woods there are beautiful," Mr. Wallner was saying, his voice taking on a dreamy quality Emily had never heard from him before. "You'll see trees and amazing wildflowers they don't have up north here."

"Yay." Rich sneered sarcastically. He still hadn't touched his dessert.

Emily found herself thinking about her father. He had loved camping. Emily remembered how much fun camping trips with him had been, all the joking around, the constant laughing, the excitement of daring to try new things, the fun of staying up really late under a starry sky, talking and singing.

How warm, how comfortable, her family had been then.

Emily realized she had tears in her eyes. She quickly wiped them away with her napkin and forced herself to think of something else.

Voices around the table drifted in and out of

Emily's consciousness. "Well, I just can't go," Nancy was saying.

"Oh, come on, Nancy," Jessie urged. "Don't be such a spoilsport. It'll be great!"

Nancy rolled her eyes in disgust.

Finally Mr. Wallner stood up, indicating the end of dinner and the discussion. "I've already made the plane reservations," he said. "We're all going. And we're all going to *enjoy* it. That's an order." He laughed as he headed toward the den and his newspaper. That was a really good joke for him.

The after-dinner cleanup went quickly and quietly. Jessie tried to talk up the camping trip, but Nancy and Emily just ignored her. Finally she gave up trying and left the room.

"I'm going to flunk out because of this!" Nancy wailed.

"At least we'll be a real family," Emily said sarcastically.

Nancy stared at her, suddenly concerned. "Bitter, bitter," she said, as if thinking aloud.

"What?" Emily asked.

"Nothing. Are you okay?"

"Nancy, how can I be okay? I'm sharing a room with a deranged person!"

"Not for much longer," Nancy said, staring into Emily's eyes.

Their mother came back into the kitchen, ending the discussion.

"How come I have to carry the tent?" Rich whined, bending over in exaggerated fashion and staggering

143

along the path as if he were about to topple over on his face.

"Because it's the lightest thing we have," Mr. Wallner said impatiently, giving Rich a dirty look. "Stand up. Stop goofing around like that. This is a no-whining weekend—remember?"

"Did anyone bring the mosquito repellant?" Nancy asked, adjusting the heavy backpack on her back.

"There aren't any mosquitoes this time of year," Mr. Wallner said, leading the way through the trees. The sun had been high above them in a clear blue sky. Now it was lowering behind the trees. Shadows played over the path. The grass, still bathed in sunlight, sparkled like emeralds. Evening crept in with the shadows.

"Those are beech trees," Mr. Wallner said, pointing. "And those are poplars."

"Very interesting," Nancy said, unable to go a minute without being sarcastic.

Mr. Wallner ignored her and kept pointing out trees and shrubs. We all look very authentic, Emily thought, in our down vests and hiking boots. She shifted her pack to her other shoulder, suddenly remembering the knife, the bloodstained knife, that she had packed at the last minute.

Would she and Nancy confront Jessie with it during the camping trip?

They might.

If Jessie tried to pull something. If Jessie menaced her in any way.

"Hey, look—" Rich called, pointing, the first words he had said since they'd started their hike into the woods. A rabbit followed by two fluffy little baby rabbits scampered over the trail. But that wasn't what Rich was pointing at.

He had discovered an old cemetery just off the trail, its small, rounded gravestones leaning in all directions. A dirt road led up to the cemetery from the other side.

They hiked a little ways past the cemetery, then entered a small, grassy clearing. "The perfect camping spot," Mr. Wallner said, grinning and scratching his head. "Actually, I seem to remember this clearing. I may have camped in this very spot when I was a boy."

"Big deal," Nancy whispered to Emily, pulling off her pack and letting it drop to the ground.

Emily was a little surprised by Nancy's openly hostile attitude. She was usually better at keeping her real feelings hidden from Hugh and their mother.

Nancy used to be a great camper, Emily remembered. She used to be just about the most enthusiastic camper in the family . . . when Daddy was around.

"Hey, what's with all the glum pusses?" Mr. Wallner asked, looking at each of them. "Come on, gang. How can I get my harem into an up mood?"

His harem?

I'm going to be sick, Emily thought.

"*I'm* in an up mood," Jessie said, helping pull the rolled-up tent off Rich's back. "I'm loving this, Dad. It's really great."

"Me too," Mrs. Wallner said, although she looked tired and glad to be unloading the equipment from her shoulders.

Birds all around began to chatter as if announcing

the end of the day. The sun was sinking quickly behind the trees. The shadows brought a damp coolness to the clearing. The grass smelled fresh and dewy.

"We'd better hurry and gather firewood," Mr. Wallner said, his eyes trailing a broad-winged hawk across the sky. "Tell you what—you three girls go collect wood. Rich, Mom, and I will pitch the tent."

Nancy groaned. Jessie shouted her approval of the plan. Emily silently followed Nancy.

It was dark under the trees, and much cooler than in the clearing. "What will we carry the wood in?" Nancy asked, kicking at a clump of tall weeds.

"We'll just make a pile on the ground here," Jessie said. "Then we'll make several trips to carry it all to the clearing."

"I guess we'll need a lot of wood," Emily said, stepping into a marshy spot, slipping, but catching her balance.

"It's going to be a cool night," Jessie said. "It's pretty cold already."

They started to collect sticks, gathering an armload, then depositing it onto a big pile. A lot of the wood, they discovered, was wet, too wet to burn. They had to wander farther into the woods to find drier wood.

Stepping through clumps of tall, slender reeds, Emily bent down to examine a branch that had fallen. Maybe I can break it into smaller pieces, she thought, turning it over. She tried to crack it, but it was too thick. She broke off smaller pieces, but they were wet.

When she stood up, she couldn't see Nancy.

"Hey—Nancy?"

No reply.

"We should've brought flashlights," Emily said to Jessie, who was standing a few yards away with an armload of gray sticks.

"It got dark so quickly," Jessie said, turning her back on Emily and searching the ground for more wood. They walked together along the path.

"Where's Nancy?" Emily asked, suddenly a little worried.

Jessie didn't answer for a while, just kept walking. "I dunno," she said finally. She dropped her pile of sticks beside the path. "Let's start a new pile here."

Emily dropped her sticks onto the pile and looked for Nancy. She couldn't find her. She suddenly realized that she had lost her sense of direction.

Which way was the clearing? Were they walking toward it or away from it? Emily wasn't sure.

Something bit at her arm, a bug. She jumped, startled, and then slapped at it. She suddenly felt nervous. Jessie was a few yards away, pulling up more sticks.

Here I am in the middle of the woods, alone with her, Emily thought. She looked for Nancy, making a complete circle. But Nancy was not in view.

Jessie's been trying to kill me, first with fire, then by pushing me down the auditorium balcony. And now here we are, far away from the camp, out in the dark woods. Just the two of us.

She looked up to see Jessie staring at her strangely, intensely.

I've got to get away from her, Emily thought, suddenly overcome with fear.

I've got to slip away.

147

Jessie will kill me. Just the way she killed her friend Jolie. And then she'll come back with some lie. She'll come back to camp crying her eyes out. And everyone will believe her because she's such a good liar.

And she'll get away with murder—again.

Jessie broke eye contact. Emily had the feeling that Jessie had been reading her mind.

She knows that I know what she plans to do, Emily thought, struggling to think clearly despite her fear.

Look at her face, look at that grim expression, that fixed determination. She's planning how to do it. She's planning how to kill me.

Jessie turned away again and stepped off the path in search of wood.

Keeping her eyes on Jessie, Emily slipped behind the trunk of a wide tree, stumbling over its thick, upraised roots. Jessie bent to pick up more sticks, and Emily moved quickly.

She began walking quickly in the other direction, turning back to make sure Jessie wasn't following her. It was too dark to tell. She stopped. She heard footsteps crunching over the twigs and dead leaves.

Jessie *was* following her.

Jessie *had* read her mind. Jessie knew she was trying to escape.

Choked with fear, Emily tried to run. But the weeds were too tall, and it was too dark to see the stones and logs that littered the ground. She stumbled once, then slowed her pace.

Nancy, where are you? she thought.

How could you leave me alone in the woods with this crazed killer?

She walked quickly, kicking clumps of weeds and low shrubs out of her path. Suddenly she realized she had walked into the old cemetery. The crooked gravestones appeared much larger from this close vantage point.

She wandered in among the graves, thinking maybe she could hide from Jessie here. The ground was soft in spots. Her boots slid in the marshy mud, and for a moment she felt as if the ground were collapsing and she was about to slide down, down into one of the old graves.

A smell came up from the ground, a powerful smell of decay. Emily gasped and then tried to hold her breath. Her heart pounding, she held on to a gravestone for support and turned to see if Jessie was still following. She didn't see anyone. The gravestone suddenly made a creaking sound, tilted, and fell. She cried out and nearly toppled over with it.

"Oh!"

She backed away.

"I've got to get out of here."

She turned, trying to decide which direction to go, and nearly stumbled into an open grave. Two shovels lay beside it on the ground, forming an X, their handles crossed.

Which direction, which direction, which direction?

The moon floated up into the navy-blue sky, an eerie ring of feathery gray clouds around it. The pale light made the slanting gravestones seem to come alive, their shadows sliding and shifting.

Emily was squinting into the near distance, searching for the trail, when someone pushed her hard from behind.

Uttering a strangled, startled cry, Emily plunged forward into the open grave.

chapter

19

"Jessie—Let Me Out!"

The dirt at the bottom of the grave felt soft and wet, like pudding. Emily landed hard on her knees, sending a shock of pain up and down her legs. Then both hands hit, plunging into the thick, cold mud.

She stood up quickly, wiping her hands against her jeans.

"Jessie—let me out!" To her surprise she felt more anger than fear. "Do you hear me? Let me out!"

She could hear Jessie walking around the sides of the grave. She looked straight up, trying to see her. The eerie trails of clouds appeared to be draped around the full moon, making it look shapeless, stretched out, like a moon in a bad dream.

So this was it. Her fears about Jessie were coming true. Jessie was making her move, her final move.

I won't *let* it be her final move, Emily thought.

"Jessie—let me out!"

Emily stretched out her arms, stood on tiptoes, and grabbed the top of the grave. She tried to pull herself out, but the dirt was too soft. Clumps came off in her hands.

She dug her sneakers into the side of the grave, kicking the soft dirt free until she was standing on a low pile of it. This gave her a better grip on the top of the grave. She took a deep breath and leapt up—grabbing the graveside, using all of her arm strength to pull herself up and out.

Yes, yes.

She dug her knees into the side, scrambling up, pulling herself up.

She was almost out when the soft dirt gave way again, and she slid right back down to the bottom of the hole.

I won't give up, she thought. I won't give up.

But what was that disgusting smell? It smelled like rancid meat.

Emily looked down. The corpse of a rabbit, its fur eaten away by insects, lay at her feet. "Ugggh!" The rabbit must have fallen into the grave and starved to death.

Now I'm the rabbit, Emily thought.

She heard sounds above the grave, boots scraping against the ground. "Jessie—do you hear me?"

One more try at climbing out. She kicked more dirt onto the pile on the grave bottom. It was at least a foot high now. She stepped onto it, grabbed the top of the grave, and started to lift herself out.

Watch out, Jessie. This time I'm coming out.

She didn't see the shovel coming down on her until it was too late. Even as the metal blade of the shovel swung down onto her arm, she didn't realize what was happening.

She heard a loud crack, like someone breaking a celery stalk, and started to slip back down into the grave even before the pain arrived. The pain shot through her entire body, as if she'd been struck by lightning, and then stayed in the arm the shovel had hit, throbbing, throbbing.

On her knees in the dirt, she grabbed the arm with her other hand. But the pain was too intense. She immediately let go.

She tried to raise the arm, but couldn't. It wouldn't move. She couldn't swing it or raise it.

It's broken, she realized.

Jessie swung the shovel and broke my arm.

Now I'm helpless.

Now the terror swept over her, driving out her anger.

Jessie really does plan to kill me. And leave me in this grave.

Her entire right side throbbed with pain.

I'm trapped now. I can't climb out. I can't get away from her.

She looked down at the dead rabbit.

"No! Jessie—I'm coming out!" she screamed at the top of her lungs, screamed so hard it made her arm throb even more painfully.

The shovel swung down again, narrowly missing her head.

Emily threw herself against the side of the grave and looked up.

Another shovel swing. Another near miss.

And then, illuminated by the eerie, pale moonlight, a face peered down at Emily.

Not the face Emily expected.

Nancy's face.

"Nancy!"

Her sister glared down at her, her features frozen in grim determination, her eyes wild with hatred.

"Nancy—it's *you?*"

Emily suddenly felt so confused. Her fear mixed with hurt and surprise.

Holding the shovel in both hands, Nancy raised it high above her head.

"Nancy? What are you doing?"

Nancy stood frozen above her, the shovel poised.

"Nancy—answer me!"

Nancy glared down at her, her skin gray-green in the moonlight.

"Nancy—please!" Emily was so frightened, she didn't recognize her own voice.

Finally Nancy broke the pose. "I hate you, Emily!" she called down, her features cold, expressionless.

"But, Nancy—why?"

Nancy, still holding the shovel high, loomed menacingly above Emily, looking like a statue, a graveyard monument.

"Why, Nancy?"

"You killed Daddy!" Nancy shrieked.

She swung the shovel down with both hands.

Emily dived to the ground, and the metal grazed the top of her hair and then hit dirt.

"You killed Daddy!" Nancy repeated, her voice hoarse with hatred. "You killed Daddy! You killed Daddy! You killed Daddy!"

"But, Nancy—"

"You could've done something! You could've saved him! But you saved yourself instead!"

"Nancy, wait—please!"

The shovel came down again.

Emily rolled out of its path, landing on her broken arm, howling from the sudden explosion of pain.

"Nancy—wait!"

"You could've saved him! You lived and he didn't!" Nancy raised the shovel again.

"You took away the only two men I ever cared about!"

"What? Nancy, please—"

"Daddy and Josh! You took them both away!"

"But, Nancy, you and Josh—"

"Yes, that was me and Josh in the car the other night!" Nancy screamed bitterly. She lowered the shovel and leaned on it, glaring down at Emily with more cold hatred than Emily had ever seen in her life. "I tried to win him back. I saw you watching us—but I didn't care!"

"And—and it was you who killed Tiger?" Emily asked, her voice trembling as she began to realize the depths of Nancy's hatred, hatred that obviously had driven her over the edge.

"Of course it was me, you idiot." Nancy was

155

grinning now, as if proud of what she had done. "Why should *you* have everything? Why should everyone love *you?*"

"But, Nancy, you made it look as if Jessie—"

"Jessie was the perfect suspect, wasn't she! Right from the start. It was so easy. When she accidentally tore the head off your stupid teddy bear, I knew you'd suspect her from then on. It was so easy. I turned off the computer, then told Jessie to go ahead and use it. I doctored the shampoo. . . ."

"And started the fire at school? And pushed me down the stairs at the concert?"

Nancy didn't reply, but her smile widened. And then it was gone, replaced by an even more terrifying look of fury. "You know what, Emily?"

"What?"

"It wasn't enough."

"What?"

"It wasn't enough. You haven't paid enough."

"No, Nancy."

"You have to die, Emily. Die like Daddy."

"No, Nancy. Let me out. I can help you. We can all help you."

"I don't need help," Nancy said slowly, pronouncing each word. "You need help."

She plunged the shovel into the ground and swung a pile of dirt into the grave. "You need help, Em. I'm going to bury you now. The way you buried me."

"No, wait—"

The dirt dropped onto her head. Emily backed up until her back was against the cold grave wall. She looked up helplessly.

THE STEPSISTER

Nancy, in the eerie gray-green moonlight, was frantically shoveling now, digging the shovel blade into the dirt, heaving the dirt down into the grave.

"I'm going to bury you, Emily! Bury you, bury you, bury you . . ."

chapter

20

Six Feet Under

"Nancy—please!"

The cold, wet dirt rained down on Emily. She wrapped her one good arm over her head and ducked her head low, trying to keep the dirt out of her eyes.

"Bury you . . . bury you . . . bury you . . ." Nancy was chanting as her shovel slid into the dirt, as she frantically worked to fill the grave.

"Nancy—I'll help you! Really!"

Wasted words. Nancy, still chanting, couldn't even hear them, Emily knew.

And then suddenly the dirt stopped falling.

Silence.

And then voices above her. Shouts. Sounds of a struggle.

Emily lowered her arm and hesitantly looked up.

She could see Jessie, looking frightened. And then Jessie moved out of view and Nancy reappeared, her hair wild about her face, as if displaying her rage.

"Ow!"

"Let go!"

"Drop it!" Jessie was screaming. "Drop it! Drop it!"

Emily realized they were fighting, struggling over the shovel.

"Let go! Get away from me!"

"Drop it, Nancy! Just drop it!"

The struggle turned into a tug-of-war. Then suddenly Nancy tossed the shovel away. With a desperate animal cry, Nancy lunged at Jessie, both hands poised like tiger claws.

Emily saw the terrified look on Jessie's face as Jessie jumped out of the way. Nancy tried to pull up short, but couldn't. She ran right past Jessie. Jessie leapt up and gave Nancy a hard shove from behind.

"No!" Nancy screamed as she fell into the grave.

Emily backed away as her sister landed on hands and knees yelping in pain.

This is my chance to escape, Emily thought. She grabbed the top of the grave and, digging her boots into the muddy side, started to scramble out.

But searing pain shot through her arm and down her entire side. She fell back. Strong arms grabbed her waist.

Emily cried out and pulled out of Nancy's grasp. She backed up to the grave wall, raising her good arm in front of her, as if trying to shield herself from her sister.

"You're not going anywhere!" Nancy cried, not sounding like Nancy. Sounding like a wild animal. "Not anywhere!"

She picked up the dead rabbit and heaved it at Emily.

It made a sickening *thud* as it hit Emily on the right shoulder, sending waves of pain down her broken arm.

"Now you're dead!" Nancy roared, advancing on her sister.

Emily, her back against the grave wall, knew she was trapped. There was nowhere to go. And no way to fight Nancy off.

chapter
21

Jessie's Secret

*H*er face steady and determined now, Nancy moved forward, arms outstretched like a zombie, as if preparing to strangle her sister.

"Please, Nancy. Please! Can't you hear me?" Emily cried.

But Nancy gave no sign of recognition. She was just inches from Emily when the shovel swung down, making a nasty *clunk* as it caught the back of Nancy's head.

Nancy's eyes rolled up and she slumped to her knees, moaning in pain, her arms still outstretched.

Then her arms slowly dropped to her sides, and Nancy fell onto her side in the dirt.

"Emily—are you okay?"

Jessie leaned down into the grave.

"Nancy. She—she's—"

"She'll be okay—but what about you?" Jessie asked

with concern. There were tears rolling down her cheeks.

"Yeah. Uh . . . I guess." Emily was still breathing hard, gasping for air. "Just get me out of here—please."

A few seconds later Jessie had managed to pull Emily from the grave. They left Nancy unconscious at the bottom.

"The camp is just beyond those trees," Jessie said, pointing. "I'll run and get everyone. Just wait here."

Emily sat on the ground beside the grave, suddenly exhausted. She watched Jessie run toward the trees, then looked down at Nancy. Nancy looked so peaceful, so serene, the hatred gone from her face.

"I had no idea," Emily said to her unconscious sister, feeling the tears begin to form. "I had no idea."

"I guess my main problem was Darren," Jessie said. She tucked her legs beneath her, getting comfortable on top of the bed.

"Darren?" Emily, adjusting her cast, sat on the other bed, her back against the wall.

They had only been home one day, long enough to line up the right doctors and get Nancy into a hospital for treatment. Long enough to get Emily's arm set. Long enough to fill in their parents as best they could as to what had happened. Long enough to realize how good it felt to be home.

But not long enough to really talk to each other, which they were doing now.

"Darren is my boyfriend," Jessie explained, her

cheeks turning a little pink. "He's away at school. I can only see him during semester breaks."

"How come he hasn't been over?" Emily asked.

"Daddy doesn't approve of Darren because he's older than I am. Three years older. Big deal." She made a face. "I'm not supposed to be seeing him. Or even talking to him."

"That's why those calls late at night?"

Jessie nodded yes. "And sometimes I had to sneak out, you know, late at night. To see Darren."

"Well, that's awful that you're forced to sneak around like that," Emily said. The more Jessie explained, the guiltier Emily felt. She was beginning to realize that she had been terribly unfair to her stepsister.

"I—I guess all the sneaking around got to me," Jessie admitted. "It just made me so nervous. I'm not that kind of person. I really hated it. I was so nervous, I just wasn't myself around here. I mean, I was never able to relax. I was afraid that any moment I'd be caught and—"

"I'm so sorry," Emily said sympathetically.

"And then I was so confused," Jessie continued.

"Confused?"

"By you. I couldn't figure out why you hated me so much. Why you were always blaming me for everything, accusing me of everything bad that happened. I really thought you were crazy or something."

"I'm sorry. I really am," Emily said. "It was Nancy. All the while she was turning me against you, trying to make it look as if you were the one who— It's so awful to think that my sister blamed me for my father's death . . .

"I had a friend," Jessie interrupted, a thoughtful look on her face. "Her name was Jolie."

"I know," Emily blurted out, feeling guilty for how she had found out about Jolie.

A look of surprise crossed Jessie's face. "That was the worst thing that ever happened to me," she said softly, looking out the window. "All those horrible rumors kids started, that I'd killed Jolie. Jolie's death was an accident, a horrible accident. But just because I was the one who found her, just because everyone saw me standing there beside her body, they started saying I killed her. It was so unfair, so hurtful." Her voice caught in her throat. It took her a while to continue. "No one would believe the truth. No one. I had had a fight with her. It was over a boy, but it wasn't really important. I—I never got a chance to apologize. . . ."

"You must have felt so terrible, so alone," Emily said. She climbed off the bed with some difficulty and walked across the room toward Jessie.

"It was terrifying," Jessie said. "And now, here I was, living in this house with you, my new stepsister, and the same thing was happening to me. You were accusing me of horrible things and not ever believing me, not ever believing the truth. And all the while the truth was so sad and so different from what we thought."

Emily was unable to hold back the tears. She wrapped her good arm around Jessie's shoulder and hugged her tightly. After a few seconds Jessie returned the hug.

"I—I promise. We'll be real sisters from now on," Emily said, stepping back to wipe the tears from her eyes. "Things will be different. I promise."

Jessie started to say something, but they were interrupted by Rich, who burst into the room, carrying a book in one hand, as usual.

"It's lunchtime," he said, seeing their tear-stained faces and becoming very embarrassed that he had interrupted some kind of emotional scene. "You're . . . uh . . . supposed to come downstairs."

"How are you doing, Rich?" Emily asked, determined to be a better sister to him too. "What's that book you're reading?"

"This?" He held it up.

"Probably another one of those Stephen King horror novels he loves so much," Jessie said, shaking her head.

"No. Actually, it's a Hardy Boys book," Rich said, showing them the cover. "It's kinda cool."

"The Hardy Boys?" Emily couldn't hide her surprise.

"Wow! Things really are changing around here!" Jessie exclaimed.

Laughing together, the three of them headed downstairs to lunch.

About the Author

R. L. STINE is the author of more than a dozen mysteries and thrillers for Young Adult readers. He also writes funny novels and joke books.

In addition to his publishing work, he is Head Writer of the children's TV show "Eureeka's Castle." And he is Editorial Director of *Nickelodeon* magazine.

He lives in New York City with his wife, Jane, and son, Matt.

WATCH OUT FOR

SKI WEEKEND

A fun ski weekend turns to terror
for Ariel Munroe and her friends
Shannon and Doug!
They are stranded in a raging blizzard
and are forced to stay in a desolate farmhouse.
The people in the house are weird—and scary.
Ariel soon realizes that she and her friends
have walked into a trap,
and their only way out leads to murder!